OTHER YEARLING BOOKS YOU WILL ENJOY:

YEARLING BOOKS/YOUNG YEARLINGS/YEARLING CLASSICS are designed especially to entertain and enlighten young people. Charles F. Reasoner, Professor Emeritus of Children's Literature and Reading, New York University, is consultant to this series.

For a complete listing of all Yearling titles, write to Dell Readers Service, P.O. Box 1045, South Holland, Illinois 60473.

The Saturdays

WRITTEN AND ILLUSTRATED BY

ELIZABETH ENRIGHT

A YEARLING BOOK

Published by
Dell Publishing Co., Inc.
1 Dag Hammarskjold Plaza
New York, New York 10017

For Lisa

Yearling ® TM 913705, Dell Publishing Co., Inc.

ISBN: 0-440-47615-1

Reprinted by arrangement with Henry Holt and Company, Inc.

Printed in the United States of America

One Previous Edition

May 1987

10 9 8 7 6 5 4 3 2

CW

Contents

"IT would have to rain today," said Rush, lying flat on his back in front of the fire. "On a Saturday. Certainly. Naturally. Of course. What else would you expect? Good weather is for Monday Tuesday Wednesday Thursday Friday; and rain's for Saturday and Sunday, and Christmas vacation and Easter."

"Oh, Rush, do stop grousing," said Mona, turning a page peacefully. She wasn't even listening to what he said; all she heard was the grumble in his voice.

"But it isn't enough just to have it plain rain," continued Rush in the same tone. "Oh, no. Today it has to go and be a sousing slopping pouring wet kind of rain that you can't do anything about; not even if you put on a lot of truck like rubbers."

He was quite right. It was a very wet rain. It plinked and splashed and ran in long curly streams down the skylight. The windows were speckled and running, and occasional drops even fell down the chimney and hissed into the fire. All the city sounds that could be heard

7

above the rain itself were wet sounds; the long whish of passing automobiles, damp clopping of horses' hoofs, and the many voices, deep, or high, or husky, that came hooting and whistling out of the murky rivers at either side of the city.

"It *is* disgusting," agreed Randy wholeheartedly from the trapeze where she was sitting. "There's nothing to do!"

But Oliver took no part in the discussion for he was perfectly happy. He was drawing pictures at his own little table which had been Mona's little table first, and then Rush's and then Randy's, all depending on who was small enough to fit at the time. He was drawing with his whole being—red in the face, tongue between his teeth, feet wrapped around chair legs. It was intensely hard work. The pictures were of battleships, only they all looked exactly like teapots because they had such big spout-shaped bows and great steamy plumes of smoke coming out of the tops of them. But Oliver was very pleased with them, and whenever he made an especially good one he stuck it into the wall beside him with a thumbtack; there were about seven pinned up already.

There were four Melendy children. Mona was the eldest. She was thirteen, and had two long thick butter-colored braids that she was always threatening to cut off. Rush came next, he was twelve; dark, with mussy hair and a look of mischievous wickedness. Miranda (always called Randy) was ten and a half, with dark untidy hair like Rush's. And Oliver was the youngest, six years old; a calm and thoughtful person.

The room in which they were sitting might have been called a playroom, schoolroom or nursery by most people. But to the Melendys it was known as the Office. It was at the very top of the house so that they could make almost all the noise they wanted to and it had everything such a room should have: a skylight and four windows facing east and north, and a fireplace with a basket-shaped grate. The floor was covered with scarred red linoleum that didn't matter, and the yellow walls were encrusted with hundreds of indispensable objects: bookcases bursting with books, pictures both by the Melendy children and less important grown-up artists, dusty Indian war bonnets, a string of Mexican devil masks, a shelf of dolls in varying degrees of decay, coats and hats hanging on pegs, the leftover decorations from Mona's birthday party, and other articles too numerous to mention. In one corner of the room stood an old upright piano that always looked offended, for some reason, and whose rack was littered with sheets of music all patched and held together with Scotch tape.

In addition to various chairs, tables and toy cupboards, there was a big dingy sofa with busted springs, a blackboard, a trapeze and a pair of rings. That was all but I think you will agree that it was enough. The Melendys seemed to go on and on collecting precious

articles that they could never bear to throw away. The
Office was their pride and joy, and what it lacked in
tidiness it more than made up for in color and comfort
and broken-down luxuries such as the couch and the
piano. Also it was full of landmarks. Any Melendy child
could have told you that the long scars on the linoleum
had been made by Rush trying out a pair of new skates
on Christmas afternoon, 1939; or that the spider-shaped
hole in the east window had been accomplished by
Oliver throwing the Milk of Magnesia bottle; or that
the spark holes in the hearthrug had occurred when
Mona tossed a bunch of Chinese firecrackers into the
fire just for fun. Melendy history was written everywhere.

"There's that leak again," said Rush in a tone of
lugubrious satisfaction. "It's getting bigger than it was
last time even. Boy, will Cuffy be burned up!" He lay
staring at the ceiling. "It's a funny shape," he remarked.
"Like some kind of a big fat fish. And there're lots of
other old dried-out leaks that have funny shapes. I can
see a thing like a heart, and a thing like a baseball mitt,
and a kind of a lopsided Greyhound bus."

"You've missed Adolf Hitler, though," said Randy,
thumping down off the trapeze and lying on the rug
beside him. "See up there? That long fady line is his
nose, and those two little chips are his eyes, and that
dark place where you threw the plasticine is his mustache."

"I'm going to throw some more plasticine and make it into George Bernard Shaw," said Rush.

"Who's he?" inquired Randy.

"Oh, a man with a beard," said Rush. "I'd rather look at him than Hitler."

Mona put down her book.

"George Bernard Shaw is a playwright," she said. "My heavens, don't you even know *that*? He wrote a play called *Saint Joan*, all about Joan of Arc, that I'm going to act in someday."

"I bet that's why you were walking around your room, holding the curtain rod out in front of you, yesterday. You had kind of a moony expression and you kept talking to yourself. I thought to myself, she's gone goofy at last." Rush shook his head and laughed appreciatively.

But Mona didn't get mad. She just flapped her braids and said, "I wish you'd stop spying around. It's getting so there's no place I can practice my acting except in the bathroom."

All the Melendys knew what they were going to be when they grew up. Some of them were going to follow several professions. Mona, of course, had decided to be an actress. She could (and did) recite yards of poetry and Shakespeare at the drop of a hat. Randy was going to paint pictures and be a dancer. Rush was going to be the best pianist in the world, and a great engineer as well: the kind that builds suspension bridges, and dams, and railroads. Oliver was going to be an engineer too, but he was going to be the kind that drives trains. It was nice to have it all settled.

Meanwhile they got along very pleasantly just being children. It was sad that they had no mother, but they *did* have Father and he could not have been improved upon as a parent. And there was Cuffy; dear Cuffy, who was housekeeper, nurse, cook, and substitute mother, grandmother, and aunt. One couldn't even imagine the house without her in it. She had always been there and it seemed as though she always would be. Her real name was Mrs. Evangeline Cuthbert-Stanley, but ever since Mona at eighteen months had solved the problem with "Cuffy," she had been called nothing else. She was fat in a nice comfortable way: fat enough to creak and puff when she went up and down the stairs, but not so fat that she had no lap to sit on. She had a nice comfortable face too: wrinkles and round cheeks, and teeth as regular and gleaming as the white keys on a piano. Late at night if you had a stomach-ache or a bad dream and woke Cuffy up to tell her about it she looked different (though still nice). Her front hair was all curled up in little snails on the top of her head, while her back hair hung down in a big grey mare's-tail. Her face looked rather fallen in, and she spoke distantly as though inside a cave, because there on the floor beside her bed you could see all her beautiful white teeth grinning in a glass of water. Cuffy ruled the house. And it was an extensive domain.

Besides the Office on the top floor, there was the storeroom. Between the Office and the storeroom, as on every floor, there was a bathroom. This one served as a sort of laboratory. In it were bowls of tropical fish, Oliver's turtle, a bathtub full of damp clay, and a medicine cabinet stacked with jars of finger paint. A great swoosh of raffia hung over the towel rack. On the next floor below were Father and Rush's two rooms and below that Mona and Randy shared a room as did Cuffy and Oliver. The living room was on the first floor and so was Father's study, where through the closed door you could almost always hear the pecking and chiming of his typewriter. The kitchen and dining room were in the semibasement, and still below them was the real basement where the furnace lived, precious as the heart in a human body. It had to be watched tenderly, fed at regular intervals, cranked, shaken, and relieved of its coal gas. This was all taken care of by Willy Sloper who came in by the day and who always referred to the furnace as "She." "I got her wide open," he'd tell you on a cold night, or "Say, Cuffy, she'll be needing a couple tons stove coal tomorra, next day, tella Boss." Or oftener still with a knock on Father's study door, "Say, Mr. Melendy, the furnace, she's on the fritz again." This would be followed by an exasperated sound from Father. Once he said, "Okay, Willy. Call in Mr. Yellen. But the next time she acts up I'm going to replace her with a good dependable oil furnace; maybe gas. This way it's like being married to an Italian opera singer. Tell her I said so."

All the Melendy children had their own jobs. They each had not one but several. For instance, they made their own beds and took weekly turns at cleaning the Office (all except Oliver, of course). And the cleaning had to be thorough. Under Cuffy's eagle eye there could be no nonsense such as sweeping things under things, or shaking the mop out the window, or dusting only where it showed. It had to be well done. In addition to these there were the special jobs. Rush shined all the shoes, took care of the fuse box, repaired the radio when necessary, and was sort of plumber's assistant to Willy Sloper. Mona helped Cuffy with the mending and ironing, and had the entire responsibility of keeping the living room tidy. Randy always set the dinner table and dried the dishes, as well as sorting the laundry and making out the lists. Even Oliver had his chores. He had to water all the plants, and feed the fish and his turtle, and see that the clay in the tub was kept moist.

So between jobs and school and amusing themselves life for the Melendys rarely contained a dull moment.

This, however, was one of them.

"I'm so b-o-o-o-o-red!" groaned Randy, lifting one foot in the air and letting it drop heavily as though simply unable to sustain the weight of her boredom.

"You and me, both," agreed Rush.

"And I'm bored listening to you complain," complained Mona, slapping her book together.

Oliver paid no attention to any of them. "Why don't we play something? Parcheesi or something?" suggested Mona.

"Oh, parcheesi!" scoffed Randy.

"Well, you used to like it. Then how about making something out of clay, or drawing, or we might do a play."

"Clay's dreary on a wet day, and I'm tired of drawing, and it's no fun being in plays with you, Mona, because you take all the leading parts, and Rush and I are only the fathers and mothers or the maids or the policemen or something."

"Oh, all right, you're impossible!" Mona retired to her book. "Why don't you read?"

"I've read everything," said Randy, which wasn't true, but she was enjoying being difficult. It was a novelty.

"The radio's busted again, I suppose. I could fix that," said Rush, and got up. But instead he went to the piano and stood there, one hand in his pocket, and his other hand skipping over the keys, jigging out a neat precise little tune that they all knew.

"And for heaven's sake don't play Bach," ordered Randy. "It's so *jumpy* for today."

Rush slung his leg over the piano stool and sat down. With both hands he began to play slow deep chords that fitted together into a wonderful dark mysterious music.

"Yes, that's better for today," approved Randy. "What is it anyway?"

"Bach," said Rush without turning his head. "Just shows how much you know about music."

"Not an awful lot," admitted Randy humbly.

"Not any," said Rush.

He played another bar.

"Not many people your age do, though," he added kindly. "Gee! I wish I had enough money to go to Carnegie Hall and hear something good. Schnabel or somebody."

"You got your allowance today," said Mona. She could read and listen at the same time.

"Fifty cents isn't enough," said Rush. "And besides I need some shoelaces and a new writing pad and I owe a dime to a guy at school."

Randy sat up on the hearthrug and stared into the fire. There was one little fitful pale-blue flame among all the golden ones in the grate.

"I have an idea," she said slowly.

Mona went on reading. Rush went on playing. Oliver went on drawing his fourteenth battleship.

"I think I have a good idea," repeated Randy patiently, and they looked at her.

"Well?" said Mona, her finger in her book.

"Let's start a club!" suggested Randy.

"Oh, look at all the clubs we've had already," said Rush. "The Mystery-Solving Club. The Tropical Fish Collectors Club. The Helping-Cut-Down-the-Electric-Light-Bill Club. What ever happened to any of them? They were all the same. Mona was always president and we never had more than two meetings."

"But this one will be different," persisted Randy. "Listen, Rush. Each of us (except Oliver, of course) gets fifty cents allowance every Saturday. Now. You want to go to Carnegie Hall and hear some music. Mona wants to go to a play. I want to see those French pictures Father was talking about. Every single one of those things costs more than fifty cents. Now what I was thinking was this. We're all old enough to be allowed to go out by ourselves—except Oliver—if we promise to be careful and not get run over or talk to people or anything. So why don't we put all our allowances together once a week and let one of us spend them? I mean, for instance, Mona would get a dollar and a half next Saturday and she could go to a play. Then the next week you'd get it, and the week after that it would be my turn. See? Only one rule would be that we couldn't save it, or just spend it on things like candy or a movie. We'd have to do something really good with it; something we'd always wanted to do."

"Say, that's not a bad idea at all." Rush looked excited. "We could pool our resources—that's what it's called, pooling your resources. Gee whiz, that would mean a dollar and a half for each of us if we pooled our resources!"

"We'd have to ask Father," said Mona.

"Oh, he'd say yes. He believes in children being independent."

"We'd have to ask Cuffy."

"Well, if we asked Father first and he said yes Cuffy would say yes too. You know she would."

"And what about shoelaces and pads and the dimes we owe?" Mona meant to find every flaw in the plan before she was won over. "There are always things like that."

"We'll just have to be careful," replied Rush.

"And there's always the Pig if necessary."

They all looked at the big painted Mexican pig bank on the bookcase. He was full of undigested pennies and nickels: so far nothing had ever justified emptying him.

"I couldn't bear to break him," mourned Randy.

"I think we could get enough out just by jiggling him upside down. And by kind of helping the pennies out with a nail file," supplied Rush.

Mona gave him a look. "You sound as if you'd tried it already."

"Just once," admitted Rush. "Just to see how much there was. I put it all back in again though. There was seventy-nine cents then, and I bet there's a lot more now."

"I don't know, Randy." Mona was beginning to look excited too. "Maybe it is a good idea."

"Good? It's swell!" boasted Randy happily. "But we have to think of a name for the club."

"We could call it The Pig if Necessary Club," suggested Rush.

"Or the Pooled Resources Club," said Mona, with a withering glance. "Why not just The Saturday Club?"

"That sounds like a lot of dressed-up grown-up ladies listening to Tchaikowsky," objected Rush. "Let's see. I know! We can call it The Independent Saturday Afternoon Adventure Club. In front of people we can speak of it by its initials. I.S.A.A.C. Get it? It sounds just like the name Isaac and nobody will ever catch on!"

"Oh, Rush, I think that's really good!" cried Randy enthusiastically, and even Mona was forced to agree.

"I want to belong," said Oliver unexpectedly, in a loud firm voice.

"Belong? But, darling, you're too young," said Mona. "You won't be allowed to go out by yourself for at least four years."

"And you only get ten cents a week," Rush reminded him a little unkindly.

"That's all right," persisted Oliver doggedly, "I can go out with Cuffy. I'll give you my ten cents each week· so I won't be able to spend it. And then when it's my turn you can each give me my ten cents back. Then I'll

have four dimes and I can go to the dime store and get
a whole set of field artillery."

Rush looked at him in awe. "Not bad figuring for a
kid your age." He turned to Randy. "I make a motion
we let him join."

"Of course he'll join!" responded Randy warmly. And
she went over to give Oliver a big hug which he avoided
neatly by putting his head under the table.

"Listen!" said Mona, looking a little self-conscious.
"Is it all right if we do anything we want to? I mean,
if I want to do something more than go to a play, can
I do it?"

"I don't see why not. And you can even keep it a
secret if you want to. Can't she, Rush?"

"Okay by me," said Rush. "Maybe I'll go to the Met-
ropolitan Opera House instead of Carnegie. Maybe I'll
take a ride to Staten Island, or go up on top of the Empire State Building. Maybe I'll buy a set of trained fleas.
Who knows? A dollar and a half is no paltry sum."

"And my dime," Oliver pointed out.

"And your dime, Fatso, my friend," said Rush. "That
makes a dollar sixty and I think it's swell of you to want
to do it."

Oliver began putting his paint things away. It was
dusky in the big room. The skylight glowed with a pale
reflection of city lights, and the fire had burned to em-
bers in the grate. Outside the rain whispered and mur-

mured against the glass, as though the air were full of secrets. Rush went back to the piano, playing softly, absent-mindedly, thinking about his Saturday and the way he would use it. Mona lay face down on the sofa, and Randy sat cross-legged on the hearthrug. They were thinking too.

A piercing sound shattered the peace of the moment: Cuffy was blowing the police whistle down in the kitchen. That meant it was time for Oliver's supper, time for Randy to set the table, time for Rush to get to work on the shoes, and for Mona to tidy up the Office, since it was her week. And it also meant that it was time for Father to stop working. If he didn't Cuffy would come up to the study and stand at the door saying gently but firmly, "Now, Mr. Melendy, it's half past five. You've been working a long time. You ought to get a little rest for yourself." And there she'd stand till Father was forced to give in.

Mona snapped on the lights.

"All right, kids, beat it," she said. "I'm going to pick up."

Oliver and Rush ran down the stairs: Oliver galumphing like a baby buffalo, and Rush so quickly and lightly that you hardly heard him.

Randy went into the bathroom in a daze and washed her hands in cold water (it took forever for the hot water to get up to the top floor). She was thinking when my

Saturday comes what will I do with it besides the pictures? I mustn't waste a minute or a penny of it.

It was like a door opening into an enchanted country which nobody had ever seen before; all her own to do with as she liked.

SATURDAY TWO

O F course Father said yes. But he had certain conditions which they already knew by heart. They were the same ones he had imposed when they started going to school by themselves.

"Don't get run over," he said. "That's the first and most important rule. Look where you're going, and watch the lights when you cross the street. This applies to Randy in particular who believes too often that she's walking in another world: a safer, better one. It's the people who make the safety on this earth as well as the trouble, unfortunately." Father glared at the newspaper that lay on the floor beside him. "Sometimes I think the Golden Age must have been the Age of Reptiles. Well, anyway, let me see what was I saying—? Oh, yes. Randy and the lights. And another thing. If you get lost or in trouble of any kind *always* look for a policeman. Sooner or later you'll find one and he'll know what to do; and don't hesitate to ask him even if he's the traffic cop at Forty-second and Fifth with busses breathing fire on every side. Let's see, what else?"

"Don't talk to strangers," Randy prompted him.

"Yes, that's right, don't talk to strangers. Unless you know by looking at them that they're kind people, and even then think twice. Be home no later than quarter to six, and Randy had better make it five." He picked up his newspaper and flapped it open. "That's about all. Oh, one last thing— See that you do something you really *want*; something you'll always remember. Don't waste your Saturdays on unimportant things."

"Yes, that's one of the rules," Mona told him.

"Is it? Good. Then go with my blessings."

Then they went to Cuffy who naturally said yes too, but not as if she cared for the idea.

"Well, I hope it's all right, I'm sure. Seems to me like you're pretty young to be kiting all over a big city by yourselves. And one at a time, too, not even together. Don't you get run over now!" They couldn't help laughing at that: all grownups had learned the same set of precautions apparently.

"And it's nothing to giggle about, neither," said Cuffy severely. "I don't want nobody run over, nor nobody lost so's we have to get the police out after 'em. I suppose I can't keep you from getting a little lost once in a while. It'd be against nature. But not so lost that we have to get the police out after you."

Good old Cuffy. It was that sort of thing that made them love her so much.

"If you *do* get lost," she continued, "you can always go up and ask—"

"A *policeman!*" shouted Mona and Randy and Rush in unison.

"Do you think it's polite to take the words right out of people's mouths?" inquired Cuffy, pretending to be offended. "And another thing—"

"DON'T TALK TO STRANGERS!" they cried.

"Well," said Cuffy, giving up. "I can't say much for your manners but I'm glad to' see you've got the right ideas at least."

"What about strange policemen?" said Rush, looking innocent.

"Oh, go on with you! Out of my kitchen, the whole tribe of you!" Cuffy made sweeping gestures with the broom. "My patience is worn about's thin as the sole of my shoe."

But that wasn't true, and they knew it. Cuffy's patience was as deep as the earth itself.

After a brief discussion it was decided that Randy as founder of the Club should have the privilege of the first Saturday. For the next five days she worked feverishly in her school craft shop whenever she got a chance, and by Friday evening she was able to distribute four small pins cut out of copper, and each bearing the mysterious name Isaac.

"Swear on your sacred word of honor *never* to tell anyone what this pin means," Randy said to the Club members. And they all swore, even Oliver. It was a solemn moment.

Saturday dawned much the same as any other day, maybe even a little greyer than most, but when Randy woke up she had the same feeling in her stomach that she always had on Christmas Day. A wonderful morning smell of coffee and bacon drifted up the stair well from the kitchen, and she could hear a familiar clattering spasm deep in the house: Willy Sloper shaking down the furnace. Mona was still asleep, a mound entirely covered up except for one long trailing pigtail that looked as if it were awake all by itself.

Randy lay staring absently at the wall beside her bed where pictures hung at haphazard intervals. She had painted all the pictures herself and there was a reason for their strange arrangement: the wallpaper was old and the pictures served to cover up peeled and faded places. They were all drawings of enigmatic-faced princesses and sorceresses. Each had mysterious, slanted eyes, a complicated headdress and elaborate jewels; each was posed against a background of palaces, rocks and dashing waves, or forests with unicorns. "Don't you ever get tired of drawing Lucrezia Borgia all the time?" Rush had once asked her.

For a while Randy lay still just being happy; then she stretched. S-t-r-e-t-ch-ed way up and way down. During it she probably grew half an inch. After that she got out of bed, stepping over her bedroom slippers as usual.

"Ow! Is it cold!" Randy complained happily, and closed the window with a crash that drew protesting grumbles from the little mountain range that was Mona.

The morning finally went by with Randy pushing it every second. It was awful to sit at the lunch table while Cuffy calmly insisted that she must eat everything on her plate. Everything.

"Oh, Cuffy, even my beets?"

"All your beets," replied Cuffy inexorably. "And all your squash."

Randy looked witheringly at the food on her plate.

"Beets are so boring," she said. "The most boring vegetable in the whole world next to squash."

"Not so boring as spinach," said Rush. "Spinach is like eating a wet mop."

"That will be enough of that!" commanded Cuffy in the voice that meant no nonsense.

At last it was over, even the tapioca, and Randy just stopped herself in time from remarking that she considered tapioca the most boring dessert in the world next to stewed rhubarb.

Mona came into their room while Randy was changing her dress.

"How'd you like to borrow my ambers?" she asked.

"Oh, Mona!" Randy was overcome. "Do you mean you'd let me? Honestly? Oh, I'd be so careful of them, I promise I would."

She felt like a princess in her brown velveteen dress

with the amber necklace that had belonged to Mother. "It's like big lumps of honey," she said, staring into the mirror.

"Well, don't you lose it now," admonished Mona, not quite regretting her generosity. "Have a good time, Ran, and don't forget you have to be back by five."

"I won't," promised Randy, giving her sister a hug. "Good-bye, you're swell to let me wear the ambers."

She said good-bye to everyone just as though she were going away for a long voyage. Cuffy gazed at her thoughtfully.

"You look awful little to be going off by yourself like this," she said. "Now remember, don't you get run over and don't—"

"I won't, I won't!" cried Randy, quickly running down the steps and waving her blue leather pocketbook in which the dollar and sixty cents rattled wealthily.

My, it's a nice day, she thought. Nobody else would have thought so. The sky was full of low clouds and the air had a damp, deep feeling in it that meant rain after a while. But being by yourself, all by yourself, in a big city for the first time is like the first time you find you can ride a bicycle or do the dog paddle. The sense of independence is intoxicating. Randy skipped halfway up the block, a leisurely lighthearted skip, and then she walked the rest of the way, stepping over each crack in the pavement. It was very dangerous, she had to be careful, because if she did step on a crack she would be turned into stone forevermore.

In Fifth Avenue the big green busses rattled by like dinosaurs. I'm going to walk though, Randy decided. I'm going to walk all the way and look in all the windows. So that's what she did. The shop windows were wonderful: Woolworth's dime store was just as wonderful as Tiffany's jewelry store, and she reached Fifty-seventh Street in either a very long or a very short time, she wasn't sure which, because the walk had been so interesting.

It was just beginning to rain when she came to the art gallery where the French pictures were being shown for the benefit of war relief. It cost seventy-five cents to go in, so Randy planned to stay a long time and gave her coat to the doorman.

The gallery was hushed and dim after the bright, sharp street. The soft rugs on the floor, the soft neutral color of the walls, with each picture glowing beneath its own special light, made her feel as if she had walked into a jewel case.

"Catalogue, miss?" said a man at a little desk. His eyeglasses flashed in the dimness.

"Thank you," Randy said, and took one of the little folders he offered; then, almost on tiptoe, she stepped into the main room of the gallery. There were a lot of people looking at the pictures and talking to each other as if they were in church, low-voiced and serious.

One of the people she knew, and at sight of her Randy's heart sank. It was old Mrs. Oliphant ("the Elephant," Rush called her behind her back) who really was old because she had known Father's father way back in the last century. She was a big, tall old lady with a lot of furs that smelled of camphor, and a great many chains around her neck that got caught on each other. Now and then she came to the Melendys', and once they had all been taken to Sunday dinner at her house when it was raining and everybody ate too much and Oliver got sick on the bus going home. She was nice, Randy supposed, but so far away in her oldness and dignity. She hoped Mrs. Oliphant wouldn't notice her.

Pretty soon she forgot about everything but the pictures. There was a nice one of a girl in an old-fashioned dress playing the piano. She had a snub nose and a long yellow braid sort of like Mona (only of course it was probably a French girl). If she looked at a picture long enough, without being interrupted, Randy could make it come alive sometimes; and now she could almost hear the music the girl in the picture was playing: quite hard music, probably, but played very stiffly, with a lot of mistakes, the way Mona played.

"Marvelous substance," murmured a hushed voice behind her, and another hushed voice replied, "Unbelievable resilience in the flesh tones!"

Gee whiz, thought Randy, are they talking about the picture? And she moved on to the next one; a field all

burning yellow in the sunshine. You could tell it was
twelve o'clock noon on a summer day; probably July.
Randy could nearly smell the heat, and hear the locusts
in the trees sounding exactly like Father's electric razor
in the mornings. She was having a good time. She
looked at all the pictures: fat ladies bathing in a brook,
a girl with opera glasses, apples and pears on a blue
plate, a man in a boat, two dead rabbits, and then all
of a sudden she came to the picture that was hers, her
very own one.

Randy was always finding things that belonged to her
in a special way, though ownership had nothing to do
with it. Now she had found the picture. The catalogue
told her that the picture was called The Princess, that
it had been painted by someone named Jules Clairon
in the year 1881. In the picture a girl about Randy's age
was sitting on a garden wall and looking out over an
enormous city. She had a solemn little face: her long
hair hung to the sash of her old-fashioned dress, and her
high-heeled boots were buttoned almost to the knee.
Among the potted chrysanthemums at her feet sat a
black poodle with a red bow on top of his head. On
either side the clipped plane trees were almost bare, and
in the distance the huge city was spread in a dusky web
of blue and grey.

It was easy to make this picture alive. Randy stared at
it fixedly, hardly breathing, hardly thinking, and pretty
soon she thought she could smell the mixture of damp

earth and burning leaves and smoke from distant chimney pots; she thought she could hear the hum of the city and the clear voices of children somewhere out of sight. A day had come and gone, years ago, and still it was alive. I wish I'd known that girl, Randy thought.

She felt a touch on her shoulder that brought her back to her own world with a start. On her shoulder she saw a knuckly black glove, and against her cheek she felt the prickling of camphory fur. The Elephant, darn it, thought Randy crossly. Just when I was getting right *into* that picture, too.

"Well, well! Why, Mona dear! What are you doing here?" inquired Mrs. Oliphant in her deep cavernous voice with its faint foreign accent. "Or is it little Miranda?"

"Miranda," replied Randy politely, with a smile that was nothing but stretching the corners of her mouth.

"Of course, of course. Mona is the one with the hair," said Mrs. Oliphant, whacking Randy's shoulder absentmindedly. "You seem very interested in this picture, Miranda."

"I think it's beautiful," Randy said, sloping her shoulder out from under Mrs. Oliphant's hand as tactfully as she could.

"It isn't so beautiful as I remembered it," observed Mrs. Oliphant, regarding it with a frown. "But then I haven't seen it for sixty years. Not since I was eleven years old."

"Eleven years old!" repeated Randy. It was impossible that Mrs. Oliphant had ever been eleven. "Not since the day it was finished," the old lady explained. "You see, I was the girl in the picture."

"You!" cried Randy, amazed. Her mouth dropped open half an inch.

"That's I at the age of eleven," said Mrs. Oliphant, very pleased at Randy's surprise. "Not much to look at, was I?"

"I think you looked nice," Randy considered the girl in the picture. "Interesting and, well, nice. I was just wishing I'd known that girl."

"And how she would have loved knowing you. Sometimes she was very lonely," said Mrs. Oliphant. "Unfortunately she disappeared long, long ago."

Randy looked up at her companion's face. What she said was true. The face was so old, crossed with a thousand lines, and the dark, fiery eyes were overhung by such severe black brows that every trace of the little girl she had once been had vanished with the past.

"What was that big city in the distance?"

"It was Paris," said the old lady, with a sigh.

"Who was the dog?"

"Tartuffe, we called him. He was a selfish old beast, and very dull company." Mrs. Oliphant shook her head and laughed, remembering. Then she looked about her questioningly. "Who is with you, Miranda? I don't see any of your family."

"I'm all alone," Randy told her.

"Alone? How old are you, child?"

"Ten," said Randy.

Mrs. Oliphant shook her head again. "When I was your age such a thing was unheard of. My aunts would have fainted dead away at the suggestion. What a lucky girl you are!"

Randy agreed. Really, I am lucky, she thought.

"Well, since we are both alone," suggested the old lady, "why don't you come with me and have a cup of tea, or an ice-cream soda, or a chocolate marshmallow walnut sundae, or whatever you prefer?"

Randy was beginning to like Mrs. Oliphant very much. "I'd love to," she said.

Surrounded by an aura of camphor and eau de Cologne, and with all her chains jingling, the old lady swept splendidly from the gallery. Randy followed in her wake, like a dinghy behind a large launch.

Outside the moist air had become moister. A fine mist was driving down. Mrs. Oliphant disentangled an umbrella from her handbag and the tail of one of her furs. When it was opened the umbrella proved to be extremely large and deep. They walked under it, close together, as under a small pavilion. "I've had it for twenty-five years," Mrs. Oliphant told Randy. "It's been lost once on a bus, twice on railway trains, and once at the London Zoo. But I always get it back. I call it the Albatross."

After they had walked a block or two, they came to
a large hotel which they entered, and the old lady,
having checked the Albatross, led Randy to a large room
full of little tables, gilt chairs, mirrors, and palms in
fancy pots. At one end of the room on a raised platform
there was a three-piece orchestra: piano, violin, and
cello. All the musicians looked about fifty years old.

A waiter who looked old enough to be the father of
any one of the musicians led Mrs. Oliphant and Randy
to a table by a long window. After a period of deliberation, it was decided that the old lady would have tea
and toast, and Randy would have vanilla ice cream with
chocolate sauce.

"And, François, bring some petits fours, also."

"Parfaitement, madame," said François, creaking
agedly away in the direction of the kitchen. Randy did
not know what "petits fours" meant, but she did not
like to ask.

"Ah, yes," said Mrs. Oliphant when she had uncoiled
from her layers of furs, taken off her gloves, untied her
scarf, and arranged her necklaces. "My childhood was a
very different thing from yours."

"Tell me about it," said Randy. Then "please," as an
afterthought.

"Would you like to hear the whole story?"

"Yes, yes, please, the whole story," begged Randy,
giving an involuntary bounce on the hard chair. She
loved to be told stories.

"Well, it's a long time ago," said the old lady. "Before you were born, even before your father was born, imagine it! The garden in the picture was the garden of my father's house in Saint-Germain near Paris. It was an old house even then, tall and narrow and grey, with patches of ivy. The inside of it was stuffy and dark and full of furniture. When house cleaning was going on, all the windows were opened; never any other time, and I can remember the smell of it to this day: the mixed odors of cloth and cough medicine and age. I was the only young thing in the house, even Tartuffe, the dog, was older than I. My mother had died when I was born and my father's business kept him in Paris all day, so I was brought up by my aunts and an English governess. They gave me my lessons too, I was never allowed to go to school. The aunts were all maiden ladies years older than my father. They always wore black, took pills with their meals, worried about drafts, and spoke in quiet polite voices except when shouting at Tante Amélie, the deaf aunt, who carried a great curved ear trumpet like the tusk of an elephant. Ah, here is the tea."

François arranged the feast before them. Petits fours turned out to be the most wonderful little cakes in frilled paper collars: pink, and pale yellow, and chocolate, with silver peppermint buttons on top. Randy's eyes glittered with such enthusiasm that the old lady was delighted. "You shall have some to take home to the other chil-

dren. François, please bring us a boxful of petits fours
to take home."

"That will be wonderful," Randy said, not quite with
her mouth full, but almost. "Please tell me some more."

"Very well," said her friend. "The English governess
was also a spinster, also elderly. Her name was Miss Buff-
Towers and she was related in some way to an earl, a
fact she was very proud of and never forgot. She had
long front teeth, the color of old piano keys, and a huge
coiled arrangement of braided hair on top of her head
like an orderly eagle's nest. She was a kindhearted creature but she knew as much about raising children as I
know about raising coati-mundis. (I'm not even sure
what they are.)

"You can see that my life was far from exciting. I
knew no children, rarely left my own home at all. If it
hadn't been for the garden I might have gone mad from
boredom.

"This garden was very large, enclosed by a high wall,
and shaded by old chestnut trees that bloomed every
spring in great cornucopias of popcorn. There was a tiny
bamboo jungle, and a summerhouse with a wasp's nest,
and a little lead fountain, and two enormous mossy
statues: one of Diana, and one of Apollo. At the end of
the garden the wall was low enough to permit seeing
the magnificent view of the city. In the distance the
whole of Paris lay spread out like a map: golden in the

morning, blue in the dusk, shining like a thousand fires
at night.

"I spent all the time I could in the garden. I had a
swing there, and many hiding places for myself, my
dolls, and Tartuffe. I used to take my lessons to the wall
at the end, looking up from my dull books every other
minute to see the city far beyond. I never tired of looking at it and wondering about it.

"One September evening when I was eleven years old
I had gone into the garden, and was sitting in my usual
place on the wall looking at the city and hoping dinner
would be ready soon. I heard steps on the little gravel
path behind me and, turning, saw my father and another
gentleman, a friend whom he had brought home for
dinner. I stood up respectfully and was introduced to
Monsieur Clairon. He was a tall man with a brown
beard and pleasant eyes. I had a feeling, looking at him,
that he was more alive than most people.

" 'Your daughter makes me think of the princess in a
fairy tale who looks out of her tower at the world,' he
told my father. 'Someday I would like to paint her just
as she was: sitting on that wall.'

"I was flattered and self-conscious, but only for a
moment.

" 'We mustn't make her vain, Jules,' said my father
in a stately voice. 'That plain little face was never meant
for Art.' Dinner, for once, was fun. Monsieur Clairon
told jokes and stories, everybody laughed, and each story

was repeated in loud brays for Tante Amélie with the greatest good will.

"'I've been making sketches at the carnival down the street,' he told me. 'I can never resist carnivals. This one has a camel and a dancing bear as well as the usual carrousel and fortunetellers. It makes good pictures. You've seen it, I suppose, mademoiselle?' He turned to me.

"'No, monsieur,' I said sadly. I knew there was a carnival somewhere in the town. Bursts of music had been drifting over the wall all day.

"'But you must see it!' Monsieur Clairon insisted. 'It leaves at midnight. I should be happy to take you this evening—'

"'Heaven forbid, Jules,' said my father, with a distressed smile. 'Gabrielle would come home with smallpox or whooping cough or measles or all three.'

"'And so *dreadfully dirty!*' added Miss Buff-Towers.

"'Someone might even kidnap her!' said my Tante Marthe, who always expected the worst.

"'It's out of the question,' stated my father firmly.

"For the first time since I was a tiny child I dared to defy the collective opinion of my aunts, father, and governess.

"'But I want to go!' said I, laying down my fork. 'I want to go *terribly!* Why can't I? I'll wear gloves and not touch anything, I promise. When I come home I'll gargle. Please let me go, please please please!'

"My father stared at me. Even his eyebrows and mustache looked annoyed.

" 'That will be enough, Gabrielle,' he said.

" 'You never let me go anywhere!' I persisted. 'I've never seen a carnival. Or a real live camel. Or a dancing bear. I'd like to see something besides just this old house all the time!'

"My father's face was dark as the wine in his glass.

" 'Go!' he roared. 'Upstairs, immediately! Without dessert!'

"And up I went, crying into my sleeve and hearing above my sobs the turmoil in the dining room: Monsieur Clairon interceding for me, my father expostulating, and above that the loud, toneless voice of Tante Amélie saying, 'What's the matter? Why is Gabrielle crying? Why doesn't someone tell me something?' And Tante Marthe bellowing into the ear trumpet: 'GABRIELLE HAS BEEN A VERY NAUGHTY GIRL!'

"After I had gone to bed and Miss Buff-Towers had heard my prayers, and wept a few embarrassing tears over my disobedience, I lay in bed very still and straight and angry. Through the closed window I could hear rowdy strains of music.

"At last I got out of bed and opened the window which looked out over the garden and the distant lighted city spread like a jeweled fabric. For the first time I was sorry that my room was not at the front of the house since then I might have glimpsed the carnival.

The music sounded gayer than ever, and I could hear bursts of laughter above the noise. Slowly my anger turned to curiosity and active rebellion. An adventurous flame sprang to life within me. Quickly in the dark I dressed in my oldest dress. Quickly I stuffed the bolster under the blankets just in case someone should look in. But money! I wanted to ride on the carrousel and to see the dancing bear. There were only twenty centimes in my pocketbook, and then I remembered the gold piece! My father had given it to me on my last birthday; at the time I had been disappointed, but now I was glad. I took it out of its box, put it in my pocket with the twenty centimes, and cautiously opened the door to the hall.

"The fat bronze goddess on the upstairs landing was brandishing the gas lamp like a hand grenade. Downstairs I heard my father shout, 'Why don't you move your queen?' and knew that he was playing chess with Tante Amélie. I turned back to my room and closed the door behind me. Nothing was going to stop me now. I went over to the window and opened it again. Aged ivy covered the walls at either side, and, scared to death, in my clumsy old-fashioned clothes, I reached out among the leaves till I felt a strong stem like a cable, stepped over the iron grille in front of the window, and with a breathless prayer, began my descent. Very awkward it was, too. I made a lot of noise, and all the sparrows in the ivy woke up and flew chattering away. About six feet above the ground the ivy ripped away from the wall, and down I went with a crash into a fuchsia bush. I sat there listening to my heart and waiting for the entire household to come out with lanterns.

"But nothing happened! After an eternity I got up and stole out of the garden. Both the knees had been torn out of my stockings, I was dirty, and my hair was full of ivy twigs, but it didn't matter.

"In less than five minutes I had arrived at the carnival! It was even better than I had hoped: full of crowds and bright lights and noise. The carrousel with its whirling painted horses and its music was like nothing I had ever seen before. I rode on it twice and when I screamed with excitement nobody paid any attention because they were all doing the same thing. After that I bought a ride on a camel. That took some courage, as I had never seen a camel before and did not know that they possessed such sarcastic faces. Have you ever ridden on one?"

"Never," said Randy.

"You must try it sometime. It made me a little seasick but I enjoyed it. Then I went and watched the dancing bear softly rocking to and fro on his hind paws like a tipsy old man in bedroom slippers. There was too much to see; I was dazzled, and just walked about staring blissfully.

"I was fascinated by the fortuneteller's booth. It was really a large wagon with a hooped roof which you entered by a pair of wooden steps. On one side there was a large placard bearing the words: 'Zenaïda, world-renowned seeress and soothsayer! Advice and prophecy on affairs of business, or the heart. Palmistry, cards, or crystal as preferred.' On the other side there was a life-sized picture of a dark, beautiful woman gazing into a crystal globe. I hesitated only a moment, then I mounted the steps, parted the flaps of the tent, and entered. Inside the tent was draped with shabby shawls of many colors; overhead a red glass lantern cast a murky light, and at a small table sat a gypsy woman glittering and jingling with earrings, clattering bracelets and necklaces. She looked almost nothing like the picture outside. She was older, and her fingernails were dirty. I was dreadfully disappointed.

" 'What do you want, kid?' she said. Her voice was hoarse and rough as though she had spent her whole life shouting.

" 'To-to-have my fortune told,' I stammered.,

" 'Got any money?' asked the woman doubtfully, looking at my torn stockings and dirty dress.

" 'Yes,' I said.

" 'Let me see it,' she demanded.

" 'I brought the gold piece out of my pocket. The gypsy examined it craftily; then she smiled a wide, delighted smile. One of her teeth was black.

" 'You must have found that in a well-lined pocket,' said she.

"At first I did not understand what she meant. Then I was angry.

" 'I never stole anything in my life!' I told her. 'My father gave it to me for a present.'

" 'Your father? He is a rich man?'

" 'I suppose he is,' I said. 'I don't know. I never thought about it. Anyway I don't think I want you to tell my fortune after all.

"Quick as a cat the gypsy sprang from her chair and barred the entrance.

" 'Forgive me, mademoiselle,' she wheedled. 'I didn't realize— Your clothes are torn and you have such a dirty face. Come and sit down; I'll tell you a fortune you'll never forget: splendid, wonderful things are going to happen to you. I see luck shining all around you!'

"Well, who could resist that? In spite of myself, I was soon seated opposite Zenaïda, my dirty hand in her dirtier one. Before she began to read my palm she called out in her harsh gypsy voice, 'Bastien!'

"A young man's face appeared at the entrance, and Zenaïda said something to him in a strange language. The young man nodded, looked at me, and burst out laughing. Then he disappeared.

"The gypsy lived up to her word. Never was such a fortune told to a human being! Jewels, lovers, fame, travels into far countries, all were promised to me, and I sat there like a half-wit believing every word.

" 'I must go,' I said at last. 'Please take what I owe

you out of this.' I gave her the gold piece trustingly. And that, of course, was the last I ever saw of it.

"We will drive you home in the wagon,' said Zenaïda, smiling. I could hear Bastien hitching up the horses outside.

" 'No, thank you,' said I. 'It's not far, only a little way. If you will give me what you owe me I will go.' I realized that the music had stopped, and a sound of hammering and clattering had taken its place. The carnival was being dismantled. I had been in the wagon for a long time.

" 'We will take you home,' Zenaïda insisted. 'It's almost midnight and we must be on our way anyhow. Where do you live, and what is your father's name?'

"Like a fool I told her.

"Bastien called to the horses, and the wagon began to move; the red lantern swinging in a slow circle overhead.

"I was so busy thinking of my glittering future that it was some time before I realized that we must have left my house far behind. When I began asking frightened questions the gypsy came close to me and grabbed my arm. She told me that I was not going home, but far away, till my father was ready to pay a price to get me back. When I cried and struggled she called Bastien and they bound my wrists and ankles and tied a rag over my mouth. All night I lay on the floor in the dark feeling the wagon lurch and sway, and hearing Zenaïda's snores and Bastien's voice swearing at the horses. I was sick with terror.

"I remained with the gypsies for three weeks. The first day Zenaïda unbraided my hair, took away my shoes and stockings, and dressed me in gaudy rags. She pierced my ears for brass earrings, and, stooping down, picked up a handful of earth and rubbed it across my face. 'There!' she said. 'Now even a gypsy would think you were a gypsy!'

"In spite of her, and in spite of the letter I was forced to write my father during the second week, telling him where to leave the ransom money if he wished to see me again, I enjoyed many things about those three weeks. The wagon and the travel and the going barefoot! The sound of rain on canvas overhead; the noise and smell of the carnival: a noise of bells and talk and music; a smell of garlic and tobacco and people and that camel! But the bad things more than overshadowed the good. Zenaïda was cruel, and so was Bastien when he got drunk, which was often.

"One fine day we came to a small town in the Loire district. There was a big cathedral on the square, I remember, that looked huge and disapproving beyond the carnival's tawdry, jingling whirl of light and music.

"When Zenaïda was telling fortunes in the wagon Bastien was supposed to keep an eye on me. I had to stay near the wagon, or run the risk of a bad whipping. But on this particular evening, Bastien, a little tipsier

than usual, went to sleep under the wagon with his head
on his hat. I saw my chance and wandered away. I had
no thought of escape. I was too dirty and dispirited, and
I had no money; my sheltered life had taught me nothing of fending for myself or what to do in an emergency.
However, for the moment I enjoyed myself watching
the familiar sights of the carnival and the many un-
familiar faces.

"Suddenly I saw something that made me gasp!

"Standing under a gas lamp at the outskirts of the
crowd was a tall man with a beard. In his hands were a
small sketchbook and a pencil. It was Monsieur Jules
Clairon who never could resist a carnival!

"I ran to him bleating like a lost sheep. 'Oh, Monsieur Clairon, save me, save me, and take me away from
here!'

"Poor man, he looked horrified, and who can blame
him? I had accumulated the dirt of three weeks.

" 'I don't know any gypsies!' said he. 'How do you
know my name?'

" 'But I'm the princess, don't you remember?' I cried
idiotically. And then I explained.

" 'Good Lord!' he said, horrified. 'I knew nothing
about your disappearance. I left Saint-Germain early the
next morning on a walking tour.

"He took me back to the house where he was staying,
and the landlady scrubbed me and gave me clean clothes,
while he got the police and went back to the carnival.

But Zenaïda must have found out what had happened, for the gypsy wagon had disappeared. Nobody ever saw it again.

"As for me, I was rushed home by train the next day. I was embraced by my haggard father, who was relieved on two accounts: first because of my safe return, and second because the ransom money had never been collected. All my aunts wept over me wetly, and I had to have my hair washed every day for two weeks, but in spite of everything I was glad to be home.

"When my father begged Monsieur Clairon to tell him how he could reward him, Monsieur Clairon replied, 'Allow me to paint the portrait of your daughter.' So that is how it came about. Later on it was he who persuaded my family to send me to school in England. I went to a convent there for seven years which, though it would have seemed dreadfully strict to you, was heaven itself as far as I was concerned."

Mrs. Oliphant opened a pocketbook like a giant clam, extracted some money to pay the bill, and clapped it shut again. "That's all," she said.

Randy rose slowly to the surface and emerged from the story dreamily.

"It was wonderful," she said. "Things like that never happen to us. We lead a humdrum life when I think about it. It's funny how it doesn't seem humdrum."

"That's because you have 'eyes the better to see with, my dear' and 'ears the better to hear with.' Nobody

who has them and uses them is likely to find life humdrum very often. Even when they have to use bifocal
lenses, like me."

It was dark when they came out. The rain had stopped
but the streets were still wet; crisscrossed with reflected
light. The shop windows were lighted too. In one bright
rectangle floated a mannequin in a dress of green spangles, exactly like a captured mermaid in an aquarium.

"I go up and you go down town," said Mrs. Oliphant
when they came to Fifth Avenue. She held out her
hand. "Thank you for coming to tea."

"Oh, thank you very much for inviting me," said
Randy. "Could I—would you let me come to see you
someday?"

The old lady looked pleased. "Do come, child. Come
by all means, and I'll show you the brass earrings
Zenaïda made me wear. I kept them for luck. I have a lot
of interesting things: Javanese puppets, and a poison
ring, and a beetle carved out of an emerald, and the
tooth of a czarina—"

"The tooth of a czarina!" cried Randy, stopping dead.

"That's another story, my dear," said the old lady ex-
asperatingly. A big Brontosaurus of a bus clattered to a
pause. "This is mine," said Mrs. Oliphant, climbing on
it and waving her hand. "Good-bye, Miranda!"

Randy crossed the street and boarded a big Stego-
saurus going the other way.

At home she went straight to Rush's room. He was

having a peaceful half hour before dinner reading, with his feet on the radiator and the radio going full blast. A voice that made all the furniture tremble was describing the excellence of a certain kind of hair tonic.

"Are you worried by the possibility of premature baldness?" inquired the voice in intimately confidential tones that could be heard a block away. "Does it trouble you to see your once luxuriant hair thinning out—"

Randy snapped off the radio. "You don't have to worry about that yet awhile," she said.

Rush looked up from his book. "Huh? Oh, hello. Have a good time?"

"Wonderful. Guess who I met?"

"Mickey Rooney," said Rush.

"No, silly. The Elephant. Only I'm never going to call her that again."

"Oh, just the Elephant." Rush was disappointed.

"Not just the Elephant. She's swell, she's a friend of mine now, and I'm going to see her. She was kidnaped by gypsies and lived with them for weeks."

"Recently?" inquired Rush, startled.

"No, no. Years ago when she was a little girl in France. I'll tell you about it after dinner. And look, she sent you these. All of you I mean."

"What are they?" said Rush, taking a bite.

"Pitty foors," said Randy. "I think it's French. For cakes, probably."

"Pitty foors," repeated Rush mellowly, through

chocolate custard. "Not bad, not bad at all. So she was kidnaped by gypsies, was she? Do you think the El— Mrs. Oliphant would care to have me come along with you when you go calling on her?"

"I know she would," said Randy. "And, Rush, let's go soon and often."

"I CAN'T say I care much for opry," said Willy Sloper after a considering silence. His voice sounded a little different than usual as he was lying flat on his back under the second-floor bathroom basin. The joint leaked. Like everything else about the house: the creaking, trembling stairs, the peeling wallpaper, and the unobliging furnace, the plumbing had lost its youthful bloom and efficiency long ago. The joints leaked, the hot-water faucets were likely to hiccup, and hot water to come out in brief scalding bursts, while the cold-water faucet in the Office bathroom could never be turned off entirely, but dripped all day and all night, like the moisture on a dungeon wall, wearing a rusty path on the enamel.

"No, I don't care much about opry," repeated Willy. "Hand me the wrench, Rush. No, not that one, the other one."

Rush, crouching by the tool kit, looked doubtfully at Willy's faded trousers and warped old shoes.

"Have you ever been to an opera, Willy? A first-class one, I mean."

"Eyetalian opry," replied Willy with dignity. "That fella Caruso I heard. Paid my money and got me a seat right up under the ceiling. From where I was settin' Caruso looked about's big as a minna, awful little fella he was, but he sure had a big voice! Whole place vibrated with it, even up where I was. And could he hold a note! Had me breathing for him double strength, he did. I thought sure he'd burst his bronickal tubes. Hand me the pliers, please."

"Gee, you were lucky," said Rush enviously. "Caruso, gee, that must have been neat."

"Well, I never forgot it," agreed Willy, sitting up red-faced and with grease on his chin. "But the resta the show was pretty trashy stuff. I'd heard mosta the tunes on the hurdy-gurdy, and the heroine, the girl he was meant to be in love with—why, for a long time I thought she was supposed to be his mother; woulda made two of him and awful homely."

Carrying the tool kit, Rush followed Willy downstairs to the next job: putty for the cracks around the pantry baseboard.

"The opera I'm going to is German," he told Willy. "*Siegfried*, the name of it is."

"I ain't no authority on German opry," Willy said. "The language don't appeal to me. What's this *Seeg-freed* about?"

"Well, it's about a guy in a forest who lives in a cave with another guy who's a gnome."

"A what?" said Willy.

"A gnome. Kind of a dwarf like Snow White and the Seven Dwarfs. Kind of a little magic guy. You know."

"Okay. Skip it," said Willy. "So what happens? Or wait a minute, Rush. You might just take a look around and see if there's any cookies first."

"That's what I like about pantry jobs," Rush said, obeying with alacrity, and being rewarded by finding the cooky jar half-full of brownies.

"Well," continued Rush between bites. "So this Siegfried makes a sword out of his father's old busted one and then he goes and kills this dragon, Fafner, and takes a magic helmet and the ring everyone's fighting for."

"Who's fighting for it?"

"Everybody. Gods and goddesses and this dwarf of Siegfried's and another one named Alberich, and giants and everybody."

"Oh," said Willy, still bewildered.

"Then he tastes some of the dragon's blood he has on his finger, and all of a sudden he can understand everything the animals and birds in the forest are saying."

"Sounds kind of loony to me," remarked Willy. "But go on."

"So this one bird tells him a lot of things, and it says

that there's a goddess named Brünnhilde sleeping on top of a mountain. There's a big ring of fire all around her, and only a hero can get through it and wake her up. So Siegfried knows he's pretty good and he climbs the mountain and gets through the fire and wakes up Brünnhilde. And then they sing back and forth about love for a little while and then it's the end."

Willy shook his head and opened the tool kit.

"What you see in stuff like that is more than I can understand."

"Well, the music's swell."

"Give me a good picture show every time," Willy said. "And there's always plenty music on the raddio. Get to work, Rush. Over there in the corner."

When Cuffy came down to the kitchen to get lunch she was outraged to find Willy and Rush conversing pleasantly over cold boiled potatoes. Willy also had a banana in one hand, and the icebox door was wide open.

"Shame on you!" cried Cuffy indignantly. "Both of you! Spoiling your lunches, and stealing the cold boiled potatoes I was saving to make hash with! Out of my kitchen!" And she brandished a ladle like a sword.

"Okay, Brünnhilde!" said Rush over his shoulder and beat it upstairs like anything. Willy was rapidly beating it downstairs at the same time.

After lunch Rush had to hurry. Randy came in as he was furiously combing his hair and trying to make it lie flat.

"What have you put on it *now?*" asked Randy, sniffing curiously.

"On what? My hair? Oh, some of Mona's face cream," grinned Rush. "I thought maybe it would make it straight. But I guess it won't."

"Mona will kill you if she finds out. You'd better go before she gets a chance to smell you."

"All right. So long, Ran."

"So long, Rush. Have a good time."

It was beginning to snow but Rush got out before Cuffy could catch him and make him wear galoshes. He had to run most of the way for fear of being late, and arrived at the opera house red in the face and out of breath. He bought a ticket in the family circle for a dollar and a half and then climbed flight after flight of stairs. They were covered with soft red carpet, but still they were stairs. Whew, I'm kind of bushed, Rush thought to himself when he had finally stepped over feet and knees to the seat that was his: number A64 —way over on the side. But he didn't care; he was lucky to have that.

After he had folded his coat and stuffed it under the seat with his cap he had time to look around. His seat was high up near the ceiling (like Willy's), so he had a good view of everything, and it was all just as he had hoped it would be: plenty of gold, and red plush, and chandeliers, and splendor. The vast curtain was golden too, and shining with a costly luster. Little black-clad musicians were beginning to creep into the orchestra pit far below like ants into a sugar bowl. Rush leaned out over the sea in front of him, opened Father's field glasses to which he had helped himself, and took a good look at the musicians. The man with the kettle drums kept tapping them anxiously and bending down to listen like a doctor listening to a heart; the violinists were talking together and gesturing either with a violin or a bow or both; and Rush watched a solemn man behind a bull fiddle open a little box, take out a pill and eat it. Above the voices of all the people in the place one could hear squeaks and scrapings, soft thumps, a toot of brass, a ripple of harp strings. Rush counted thirty-nine bald heads among the downstairs' audience. He counted twenty-six brown fur coats on ladies in the boxes.

Suddenly the lights were dimmed, and a small man came into the orchestra pit. There was a deluge of applause, the little man turned and bowed impatiently, turned back to the musicians, raised his baton, and the music began. The world faded away and was replaced by a strange legendary land of gods and goddesses and heroic adventure. The curtains parted and revealed a huge cave where a small bearded dwarf was working at an anvil. He looked exactly right, all bent double with age, and full of sly wickedness. But Siegfried wasn't exactly the way Rush had expected him to be. He sang wonderfully, of course, but he was very fat, and when he was forging the sword he looked just like a good-natured cook making a cake. Rush sat back and listened; his mouth dropped open and his foot went to sleep without his ever noticing.

After the first act was over and the singers had taken their bows the lights bloomed up all over the house, and Rush, following the crowd, found himself in an open space full of tobacco smoke and gabble. He was terribly thirsty but didn't order anything to drink at the refreshment counter as he had only a dime left. So he contented himself with five paper cups of water.

The second act was even better than the first. The scene disclosed a deep, wild forest, and the yawning black cavern mouth where Fafner, the dragon, lived. Alberich, another wicked dwarf, and the Wanderer, a god in disguise, met and sang an argument, and after a long while when they had disappeared, Siegfried bounded onto the stage with Mime, the first dwarf, behind him.

Finally the dragon came clanking out of the grotto, eyes gleaming with electric light bulbs and smoke issuing hotly from its nostrils, singing all the while in a musical bass voice. Rush, who was interested in all mechanical devices, looked at Fafner through the field glasses. Each time it sang the dragon's jaws opened and shut like a crocodile snapping at flies, and during a quiet moment a businesslike voice deep inside its stomach was heard to say, "Okay, Bill. Hold it."

The music was wonderful; swell, was how Rush

thought of it. It was made up of so many different kinds
of music. There was a music that was Siegfried's own,
and another for his sword, and another for the Wanderer, and the Forest Bird, the dragon, Valhalla, the
golden ring, and the fire. All of them were woven together mysterious and wide and deep; and each of them
came flashing out from time to time like unexpected rays
sparkling from a precious stone.

In the second scene of Act III Siegfried penetrated
the fiery circle and wakened Brünnhilde, who was clad
in glittering mail and proved to be the general shape and
size of a caterpillar tractor. It was funny how you could
forget it when she began to sing. The two great voices
mingled joyously with the great music, and at last it was
over. Thousands of hands were beaten together, and the
man next to Rush shouted a "Bravo!" that smelled of
garlic. Siegfried and Brünnhilde took repeated beaming
bows, and Rush clapped till his palms burned, thought
of yelling "Bravo!" himself, thought better of it, and disentangled his coat and cap from under the seat. Stuffing
the program in his pocket he made his way down the
many stairs, borne along in the slow, chattering tide of
the crowd. Inside his head he kept listening to Siegfried's special music. *TA* tatatatatatatata *TA!* When I
grow up I'm going to have an automobile with a horn
that plays that, he decided. Wonder why nobody ever
thought of it before?

When he came out of the opera house Rush was

astonished. The world was completely transformed: snow had been falling furiously for more than three hours, and still was. Drifts were piled high along the sidewalk, the air was dense with flakes, and Rush felt happy: this was the best snowstorm of the winter. He pushed his way past the people who were waiting for cars and taxis, turned up his collar and went out into the blizzard. In no time at all his feet were soaking wet and he loved it. He took a long time going home and made a great many detours. In the side streets the air rang with a noise of scraping as men cleared the sidewalks. All other sounds were furred with quiet by the snow; the hoots of boats came muffled from the river, cars passed noiselessly, and people walked without a sound in the feathery dusk. Rush's footsteps had a sound, though; his shoes were so wet that they squelched juicily with every step.

In East 37th Street there was a commotion. A huge long-necked machine on wheels was sucking up the piled snow along the curb. It was accompanied by a dump truck. The machine would move its long neck, turn its head, and blow the snow it had consumed into the truck, then both would move slowly along again. It's just like an animal, thought Rush, looking at the machine. Like Fafner, he thought, and began to laugh. For a long time, maybe all his life, snow machines, and threshers, and derricks, and steam shovels were going to remind him of Fafner.

Rush watched the machine for a long while, forgetting all about the time. He had companions as fascinated as himself: a man with a burnt cigar that smelled, two little kids in snow suits, a grocery boy with a cartful of packages that people were waiting for, and an old man with earmuffs. Dreamily they all progressed along the block following the machine; stopping when it stopped, and staring as if hypnotized.

"Used to take a team of hosses pullin' a snowplow to do a job like that," said the old man. "And hundreds of fellas out shovelin' the way. Nowadays they do it all by machinery. Ain't no work for nobody. That's what's the trouble with this world. I coulda told 'em."

The man with the cigar put it back in his mouth and chewed it. Rush wondered how he could.

"I suppose you prob'ly can remember the blizzard of 'eighty-eight?" he said sarcastically, around the cigar.

"Sure can," replied the old man. "I weighed two hundred and eleven pounds them days, and the wind knocked me flat as a haddock at the corner of Fifth Avenue and Twenty-third. Couldn't run the hoss cars it was so bad, and they was men diggin' all over the city. None of these here machines that only employs a couple fellas!"

The cigar man laughed a short unsympathetic laugh, more like a cough than a laugh, and departed. Rush didn't like him.

Out of the dark a woman's voice shouted: "Ernie and Walter! How many times I hafta tell you to come in?"

Ernie and Walter turned out to be the two little boys in snow suits. They left reluctantly, walking backwards most of the way and staring at the machine.

"Yessir," said the old man. "You youngsters is brought up soft. Too much machinery. Too many motors, and engines, and eelectrical deevices."

"Well, they ain't no motor on this here cart," said the grocery boy gloomily, and off he went pushing it through the snow and whistling the piercing tuneful way that only grocery boys seem to know how to do.

"Look at that, now," continued the old man grumpily, staring at the snow-removal machine. "You'd swear it was almost alive. Sometimes I think a day will come when these fellas build so much machinery that it will revolt; turn on 'em and swalla 'em up! It'll be like the days of the dinosaurs all over again: them snow machines grazin' on the snow, and Greyhound busses chargin' over the countryside with no one drivin'; and airplanes swarmin' like honeybees, and roostin' in the skyscrapers!"

"I kind of like machinery," Rush admitted. "Someday I'm going to design and build it. Engines and things. Lots of stuff."

The old man looked at him severely, and shook his earmuffed head.

"They'll swalla you up," he said. "They'll swalla you up along with the rest of civil-i-zation."

Rush's feet were becoming cold as well as wet, and he thought maybe the old man was a little crazy, so he said good night and started off in the direction of home. The old man was still talking; to himself or to the machine, you couldn't tell which.

Rush turned the corner. He began to wish he hadn't lingered so long; his teeth were chattering in his head; but just as he was about to break into a run he saw something that made him stop.

Across Lexington Avenue with its heavy traffic a dog was running. Running wildly, like a small flickering shadow, he narrowly escaped extinction beneath the wheels of two large trucks and a taxicab. "Here, pup!" yelled Rush as the dog reached his side of the street, and the taxi driver, who had missed hitting it only by applying the brakes with a tearing squeal, leaned out his window and bawled furiously, "Don'tcha know enough to keep ya dog on a lead!"

"He isn't mine," Rush tried to explain, but the cab was departing, its taillights looking indignant, and the dog was halfway up the block. Rush began to run after it. Nobody else seemed to be paying any attention, and you couldn't let a lost dog do barging around a city at night and in a snowstorm!

"Here, pup, come back," called Rush, and then he tried whistling but the dog never even paused. It turned

left into a side street with Rush hot on its heels, and when it ran down some steps into the snow-filled areaway of a vacant house Rush cornered it.

"Here, boy," he said wheedlingly. "Come on out. Come on, pup. I wouldn't hurt you."

He approached it with his hand outstretched for encouragement and to his delight the wet and shivering dog suddenly raised a front paw and placed it in the hand. Rush's heart was won forevermore.

"You're a smart guy!" he told the dog admiringly. "You come on home with me and I'll give you some supper. Come on, puppy, come on."

The dog, which had been trembling against the iron grating, made up its mind about Rush. Its tail wagged tentatively once, twice, and it gave a short conversational bark. It was a smallish dog with long ears and large melting eyes; not quite a thoroughbred face, but much better: one that was full of character. It was hard to tell what color he was, for he was so dirty and wet; his longish fur clung together in damp strings and he had no collar. Rush had never seen a dog he liked better.

"Come on, boy," he coaxed. Then he picked up the shivering stray, and held it close. All its ribs were sharp beneath his hands.

"Everything's going to be all right now," he kept saying. "I'll hide you in the cellar till Cuffy gets used to the idea; Willy Sloper's going to like you, and you'll be warm down there and I'll find you a bone too."

The boy and the dog were equally wet and dirty by this time. The snow still fell swiftly and Rush's shoes were so wet that they squelched louder than ever. The dog shivered in short, hard spasms and gave Rush's ear a lick with his warm tongue. It was a long walk home and the dog grew heavier with every block. At the house Rush hesitated. He didn't want to go in by the front door, partly for fear of muddying the carpet, but mainly for fear of meeting Cuffy or Father before he had prepared them for the dog. A glance through the kitchen window revealed Cuffy charging busily about with pot lids clashing like cymbals. The kitchen door was closed, he was glad to see. The areaway iron gate was also closed and locked, but Rush knew how he could open it; his hand was still small enough to push through the narrow apertures of the grille and turn the knob from the inside. The house door beyond was unlocked, fortunately, and presently he was tiptoeing slushily along the lower hallway toward the cellar stairs. He had a bad moment when Cuffy threw open the kitchen door and released a smell of boiled turnip and a snatch of song. "Sweet and low, sweet and low," sang Cuffy at the top of her healthy lungs. "Wind of the western sea-ea."

But she didn't come out, and quick as a thief in the night, Rush had opened the furnace-room door, pulled it to behind him, and snapped on the lights. He went tiptoe down the iron cellar steps into the great warm subterranean room where the furnace crouched glaring amid its coiled tentacles of pipe like the minotaur in the labyrinth. Rush remembered the old man with earmuffs and what he had said about the world of machines. Boy, I'd hate to be left alone with this one when it came alive, he thought; it looks like it could be mean.

At the far side of the furnace room were the washtubs. Into one of these he put the dog. Then he took off his cap and coat and jacket, letting them fall in a drippy heap on the floor.

"I hate to do this to you, pal," he told the dog, "but I want you to look handsome when Cuffy sees you. Everything depends on it. She'd never let you stay if she saw you like this." Then he rolled up his sleeves, turned on the water, reached for the brown soap and began to scrub. The dog stood without a sound, trembling wildly, and gazing with horrified eyes at Rush as if to say "This is the most awful thing that has happened to me yet!" He made Rush feel so guilty that he had to keep apologizing. "Gee, I'm sorry. Honest, I am. But it's for your own good, I promise you it is." Nevertheless, in spite of his apologies, when Rush stooped to pick up the soap which had flown from his hand, the dog with a scramble and a leap had cleared the washtub, and, covered with lather, was streaking up the stairs. Rush, scarcely less wet, went racing after him calling in a loud whisper, "Come back! For Pete's sake, do you want to get us both in Dutch?" The door at the top of the steps had not been tightly closed, alas, and the dog pushed it open and sped down the lower hall. Then there was a crash, a clatter, and a loud cry, all at the same instant, and Rush was just in time to see Randy sprawled on the floor surrounded by knives, forks, spoons, the tray, and all the salt cellars.

"Where's he gone?" hissed Rush fiercely.

"What was it anyway? Gee whiz, it came at me like a thunderbolt," said Randy, getting up.

There was no need to answer, for at that moment another loud cry issued from the kitchen. "Mad dog!" yelled Cuffy's voice. "*Mad dog!* MR. MELENDY, THERE'S A MAD DOG!"

Rush and Randy flew to the kitchen where they found Cuffy standing on a chair wild-eyed.

"Get out!" she shouted. "Lock yourselves in your rooms and call the police or the fire department or somebody!"

"He's not mad," said Rush dispiritedly—the game was up now, he knew. "Where'd he go?"

Father appeared in the doorway. "What's going on down here?" he demanded sternly.

"I tell you he's mad!" insisted Cuffy. "Covered with foam he was; I saw a dog covered with foam!"

"It's just soapsuds," said Rush sadly. "I was just washing him so you'd like him, maybe, and I could keep him."

"What dog are you talking about?" inquired Father blankly.

"Just this dog I found," Rush explained. "All wet and lost, without a collar."

Cuffy climbed down off her chair looking rather foolish.

"Where is this dog?" said Father.

"I think it's under the stove, Mr. Melendy," said Cuffy in a dignified voice. She bent down with a grunt and hauled out the miserable bundle of fur and soapsuds.

"Well!" remarked Father. "You must have seen *something* in him, Rush, but I can't imagine what."

"He'll look all right when he's clean," Rush said eagerly. "I think he's a pretty high-bred dog. I wouldn't be surprised if he's a spaniel."

"One-third spaniel, I should judge by the looks of him," said Father. "And two-thirds miscellany."

"What kind of a dog is a miscellany?" asked Randy, already on her knees by the dog.

"He means it's a mut," said Rush bitterly. Everything was awful.

Cuffy, still red in the face, opened the oven door with a clank and out came an unbearably delicious smell of chops. It was then that the dog solved the problem. Wet, unkempt, far from beautiful, he walked right over to Cuffy, turned his melting eyes upon her, and sat up on his hind paws, begging. Rush's heart swelled with as much pride as if he'd taught the dog this trick himself.

"Oh, how wonderful! Oh, Rush, how smart he is!" gasped Randy.

Cuffy frowned at the bedraggled mut and tried not to smile.

"Begging, dirty rascal!" she said, but the way she said it kindled a great suffocating blaze of hope under Rush's ribs. He looked at his father.

"He can shake hands too," he said.

"Finish washing him," ordered Father. "Then feed him. When he looks a little less like a half-drowned famine victim I can tell better. Maybe (remember I said maybe) if no one claims him in the lost and found ads, which they probably will—well, we'll see."

"Boy!" cried Rush, in a burst of gratitude.

"Boy!" echoed Randy, with a leap and two pirouettes.

"You've got to take good care of him, Rush," commanded Cuffy. "I don't want no fleas in this house. Nor no puddles on the carpets neither. Remember that! And when you're finished with that dog you go upstairs and take a good hot bath yourself!"

Rush gave Cuffy a squeeze around her ironclad waist that knocked the breath out of her.

"Gee, you're swell!" he said. "You're keen!"

"Just as long as you can get something out of me," Cuffy said, and gave him an affectionate shove. "Go on, now, get that animal out of here."

Really after he was clean and dry the dog looked very nice. He was a becoming shade of tan. The spaniel in him showed up to advantage; his ears were long and he had a feathery fringe around each paw.

"He turned out better than I hoped," admitted Father. "He even has a certain style."

Everybody was pleased with him; but Cuffy made Rush leave him in the basement while they ate supper. Rush could hardly eat, he was so excited, and of course Cuffy had to catch him stuffing bread and bones into his pockets.

"Now then," said she. "No use to smuggle things and get them pants all grease. That dog had a big supper, as you very well know. If you want bones you can come to the kitchen and ask for 'em; and remember, Rush, he's going to sleep *down cellar!*"

Nevertheless, it happened that after Cuffy was safely in bed, two feet creaked quietly all the way downstairs, and then up again with a few soft thumps and "ouches." Only the keenest ears could have heard the accompanying patter of four paws. Then all was still.

By and by there was a little tap at Rush's door and Randy came in wearing her blue-and-white striped pajamas.

"How is he?" she said.

"Look," whispered Rush. He was on the floor gazing down at the dog who lay stretched out on an old quilt with a bone beside him and his paws crossed. The pads of his paws looked very leathery and careworn, as though they had walked a thousand weary miles. As Rush and

Randy watched the dog his nose quivered nervously and he whimpered faintly from the distance of his sleep.

"See, he's dreaming," said Rush, looking as much like a doting mother as it is possible for a boy of twelve to look.

"Oh, I hope nobody claims him," breathed Randy fervently. "I'm going to get down on my knees every night until it's safe, and pray that nobody claims him. What will you name him if they don't, and you can keep him?"

"What will I name him?" said Rush. "I bet you'd never guess. First I was going to call him Siegfried, but then I changed my mind because I found him on my Saturday. I'm going to call him Isaac!"

SATURDAY FOUR

RANDY sat on her bed watching Mona get ready to go. Lunch was over and the dishes washed, but a faint odor of baked potatoes and lamb chops lingered comfortably in the house.

Mona's side of the room was covered with photographs of actors and actresses; some signed and some just cut out of magazines and thumbtacked to the wall. The most precious ones were framed and stood on her bureau with her brush and comb set, two artificial roses in a vase, and a bottle of perfume called "Night on the Nile," which had never been opened. It was all very tidy and correct. The only thing about Mona's side of the room which led you to suppose that she wasn't a young lady was her bed. It was very flat (she never used a pillow) and at the head of it sat a giant panda, made out of plush, and an ancient cloth doll named Marilyn whose face had entirely disappeared.

The sunlight came into the room and so did weaving branch shadows from ailanthus trees in the back yard.

73

Mona was brushing her hair; electricity made it stand out in a silken skein and Randy could hear it crackle like burning leaves. It was almost too bright to look at in the sun.

"You have beautiful hair," she said.

"Oh, beautiful!" scoffed Mona brushing as if she hated it. "Nasty old straight stuff. You and Rush are the lucky ones."

"Rush doesn't think so. He's always trying to make his lie down and be straight. Remember the time he put the gelatine on it?"

They both laughed.

Mona's fingers deftly plaited the golden hair. Then she put on her cleanest sweater and skirt and her green coat and hat that matched. But where were her gloves? She jerked open the bureau drawers, burrowing through them till they boiled over. Not a glove in sight. Randy got off her bed and joined the search and at last they were located in the strangest places! One in the kitchen beside the alarm clock and one upstairs in the Office on the piano.

"All my gloves behave like that," said Mona, slapping them together as if to punish them. "They never want to stay in pairs."

"They're what the newspapers call incompatible," said Rush. "What are you going to do with your afternoon? Come on, Mona, be a sport."

But Mona wouldn't tell. She patted her pocketbook

and smiled mysteriously. The truth was she wasn't sure herself.

"Good-bye, kids," she said. " 'Parting is such sweet sorrow—'."

"Scram," advised Rush, holding the door open for her, and when she had gone down the front steps he and Randy tormented her all the way up the block by yelling admonitions after her at the top of their wicked lungs. "Don't get run over! Don't get lost! Don't talk to STRANGERS!"

"I suppose I might as well practice," said Rush, slowly climbing the stairs. "Later we can go to the park." Isaac trotted at his heels. For, though Rush had honorably inspected all the Lost notices in the newspapers for the past week, he had found no description of a lost dog resembling Isaac. Poodles, yes. Dachshunds, and Sealy-hams, and Scotties, yes. But not, thank Heaven, a single mention of a small intelligent mongrel who showed traces of Spaniel ancestry.

Randy followed them. She was going to play Drug-store with Oliver in the top-floor bathroom. It was really an advanced form of mud pies. You took all the leftover tooth paste, cold cream, talcum powder, and medicines that had been hanging about the medicine cabinets long enough not to be missed, and you made mixtures. Last time they had evolved two splendid creations: Measle-not, a cure for measles made out of talcum powder, cold cream, and a dash of turtle food; and Complexion Jellyfish, a skin remedy compounded of melted soap and pink mouthwash.

Soon Randy and Oliver were happily and messily absorbed, and except for the music that poured out of the Office the house was very still.

Mona walked along the street feeling like the heroine of a play. The whole afternoon lay ahead of her filled with boundless opportunities. It was a cold day but not too cold. Mona couldn't remember when the air had ever seemed so delicious before. She felt like running, or soaring in great bounding leaps, or shouting noisily. But naturally she did nothing of the kind. She walked sedately along the street, swinging her pocketbook and smiling to herself. She wondered if the people who passed her noticed the smile and thought to themselves, Who can she be? What a strange, mysterious smile! But then (it always happened that way) she caught sight of her reflection in a glass shop window and was astonished at how much fatter and shorter she was than she thought of herself as being. Between the swinging braids her round face with its mysterious smile looked perfectly sappy. There was no other word for it. Just sappy.

Minus the smile but still happy she turned the corner to Fifth Avenue. It was full of Saturday afternoon crowds of people who had finished their work and eaten their lunch and now were busily shopping or amusing themselves. The air was filled with a big slapping shining wind and Mona saw two people chasing after their hats.

She waited on the corner till a bus bumbled to a stop in front of her, and, jumping aboard, she ran up the narrow steps to the upper deck and found a seat. The wind was terrific, it made her eyes water and her nose run; the man in the seat ahead was smoking a cigar, and great billows of strong smoke blew straight into her face. But it didn't matter. She enjoyed it all. The sidewalk was a river of people, the street was a torrent of traffic; on each side the towering buildings were studded with as many windows as there are stars in heaven, and high, high overhead against the cold blue sky a tiny airplane, flashing like a dagger, wrote a single magic word, "Pepsi-Cola," in mile-long loops of smoke.

At Forty-fourth Street Mona pushed the little bell in the railing, climbed over the lap of the stout lady who had sat down beside her, and made a perilous descent to the street.

Across the avenue, then two blocks west, and she was on Broadway! Mona had never been there by herself before, and it was wonderful! For a while she simply drifted with the crowds up one side of the famous thoroughfare and down the other. There was a lot to see and she saw most of it. She studied the pictures in front of the dazzling movie theater where a doorman in gold braid was bellowing haughtily: "Standing room onlay! Standing room onlay!" She spent an absorbed ten minutes before the doughnut palace watching a businesslike

machine creating tens of dozens of doughnuts to be
devoured by tens of dozens of hungry people. In another
machine, displayed in a drugstore, popcorn was bouncing frivolously. The whole block smelled of it. Every
place there were things to eat. In one restaurant window
a cook in a tall white cap was lifting great hanks of
spaghetti out of a vat, and in another one, farther along,
a big black woman in a green apron was frying ham-
burgers on a copper plate. Open-air stands on the corners were selling drinks made out of every kind of fruit
you can think of: orange and pineapple and banana and
coconut and papaya. But Mona was too excited to be
hungry. She just drifted along, looking and listening and
smelling. There was a lot of noise: a huge sound of
voices and footsteps, a commotion of honks and hoots
from the traffic, policemen's whistles, a noise of things
going on.

Past Fiftieth Street another window caught her attention. In it there was nothing but a lot of draped pink
silk and three wax ladies' heads mounted on stands.
Each of the ladies was smiling the same sweet stupid
smile, and each was wearing an elaborate wig: one was
blond, one was red, and one, for some reason, was lavender. On the glass in gold letters was written:

Etienne and Edward
Hairdressers and Beauty Specialists
3 items 1 dollar

Mona's heart beat fast and suddenly she knew what she was going to do. "After all, nobody ever asked me not to," she told herself. "I never promised I wouldn't." But all the time she knew that she was quibbling; the corner of her mind that never let itself be fooled was well aware that neither Father nor Cuffy would approve of what she was about to do. But nothing could stop her now, and pushing open the heavy glass door she went into the shop.

It was a busy place. People in white uniforms hurried to and fro carrying combs, scissors, bowls of hairpins: everyone was talking. The place smelled of hot hair and perfume. At one side of the room sat a long row of ladies, each with her head bowed meekly under a buzzing bell-shaped metal thing. They made Mona think of the old nursery rhyme:

> Mary, Mary, quite contrary,
> How does your garden grow?
> With cockleshells and silver bells,
> And pretty maids all in a row. . . .

Only very few of these ladies were pretty.

"Yes, dear?" inquired a voice sweetly.

There was a blond lady enthroned at a raised desk. She had a round chalk-white face with nothing in it except eyes, nose, and mouth: no wrinkles, no expression, no smile. It reminded Mona of the Tang goddess from China that Father had in his study at home. Even the lady's hair was like the goddess's headdress: it was all built up on her head in silvery-golden curls and spirals. It must be done with glue, thought Mona; I don't see how it could stay up that way otherwise, or maybe she uses gelatine like Rush. She had to smile at the thought.

"Yes, dear?" repeated the voice, this time a little more sharply. "Is there something I can do for you?"

Mona flapped her braids nervously. "My hair," she said, "I want it cut off."

The goddess never batted an eyelash. She simply turned her head and called out in a voice like an iron file.

"Oh, Mr. Edward," she called. "Oh, Miss Pearl."

Mr. Edward was tall and refined looking, with wavy dark hair and melancholy eyes like a poet. Miss Pearl was small and pretty with a smile that never left her face for an instant. She talked through it and ate through it and it was probably still there when she was asleep.

"This little girl would like her hair. bobbed," explained the goddess.

"Those lovely *braids?*" exclaimed Miss Pearl.

"Yes," said Mona firmly. "I loathe them."

"She's quite right too," agreed Mr. Edward. He stood away and regarded her through narrow eyes, more like a painter than a poet. "The little lady is definitely the subdeb type. I see a long bob; about shoulder length.

Fluffy. Soft. Youthful." He looked like a man in a trance.

"Well, take her to booth eleven, then," said the goddess practically. "Etienne's permanent wave just went home a couple of minutes ago, so it's empty."

Booth eleven was hung on three sides with silky green curtains like a little tent. On the fourth side there was a large mirror and a basin all grinning and glittering with faucets and gadgets.

Miss Pearl hung up Mona's hat and coat, draped her with a pink rubber cape, told her to sit down on the important-looking chair in front of the basin and began undoing her braids.

"Such beautiful hair, honey," said Miss Pearl. "Seems like it's almost a shame to cut it off. What'll your mamma say?"

"My mother is dead," said Mona.

"Oh. Oh, well. It sure is lovely hair, though. So long too. Way down to your hips, almost. Are you sure you want to bob it?"

"Absolutely positive," replied Mona.

"Well, okay then. Oh, Mr. *Ed*-ward," bleated Miss Pearl over her shoulder, and Mr. Edward appeared suddenly, dramatically from behind the curtain with a flashing smile, like the villain in a play. Iago, thought Mona to herself. He clicked the scissors together, hungrily; then he began. Mona discovered that her heart was beating fast again. Shining strands fell to the floor, into

Mona's lap; everywhere. In the mirror she could see her anxious face framed between a long lock on one side and a sort of ragged clump like a cocker spaniel's ear on the other.

As he worked, Mr. Edward asked all the usual dull, boring questions that Mona felt she should have outgrown long ago. Questions like what is your name, little lady, how old are you, what school do you go to, do you enjoy it, what class do you enjoy most, I bet you enjoy recess most, don't you, have you any brothers and sisters, my, my, isn't that nice, how old are *they*, and what are *their* names, etc.

Goodness, the questions children always had to answer, and politely too. Still he seemed to be a nice man, and Mona had the feeling that he was really just as bored as she was by the questions and only asking to be kind.

"Oh, dear!" cried Mona in consternation, looking at the horrible reflection of herself in the mirror. She saw a frightened face framed by a lot of straight bushy hair lopped off at the shoulders. "Oh, Mr. Edward! I look like an old English thatched cottage. I don't *like* it!"

"Now, now, never mind," he consoled her. "You just wait till we get finished. It won't look anything like this, I promise. Now, let's see—" Mona could tell that he was racking his brains for another question to ask her. Ah, he had it. "And what are you going to do when you grow up, little lady?"

Mona wished he wouldn't call her little lady, but aloud she answered politely. "An actress," she said.

"Well!" said Mr. Edward, mildly surprised.

"Isn't that cute!" exclaimed Miss Pearl, to Mona's boundless disgust. "A movie actress?"

"No," said Mona proudly. "A real actress on the stage, like Helen Hayes or Ethel Barrymore."

"Well, if that's the case we must make you as handsome as we can, mustn't we?" said Mr. Edward. "All right, Pearl, you can take over now. Good-bye, Myrna." (Mona saw that he hadn't understood her name.) "Just you relax and I'll be back in a flash."

Miss Pearl twirled the chair around and fastened a sort of metal plate to the back of it. At one end of the plate there was a curved dent that looked as though someone had taken a bite out of it.

"Just rest your neck in there, honey," said Miss Pearl. "Now lay your head back, that's right."

Cascades of warm water and foaming suds of perfumed soap flowed over Mona's scalp. Miss Pearl's fingers were light and dexterous. This was something entirely different from Cuffy's brand of shampoo. Cuffy scrubbed as if her hope of salvation depended upon it. When she was through, your eyes were red and smarting from all the soap that had got into them, and your whole skull was throbbing as though it had been beaten with a mallet. The Melendy children dreaded shampoo days as they dreaded few things, and Oliver had once been heard begging Cuffy to use the vacuum cleaner on his scalp instead.

"I used to have a couple of pigtails too, when I was about your age," remarked Miss Pearl. "I'll never forget the first time it was cut." She laughed reminiscently. "My brother cut it for me."

"Your brother?"

"Yes, my brother. The time we ran away."

"The time you ran away? From *home?*"

"Oh, if you could call it home. It's kind of like in the fairy stories: my mother died when I was a baby and a long time afterwards my father married again, but he only lived a year after that. And then there we were with a stepmother, a wicked stepmother, *just* like in the fairy stories."

"Was she really wicked?"

"She surely was. She was a mean one. Not so much to Perry—that's my brother—because he was two years older than me, and you know how boys are, kind of strong and tough. My father'd bought a new house when he married her and, my, how we hated it. It was a farm way outside of town (a little place called Verona was where we came from) and the house was kind of high and thin, made out of brick, and it had trees all around; those big, sad black evergreens; I don't know what you call them. My, I can make myself blue just remembering how the wind used to sound in the branches of those darn trees. You can sit up now, dear, we're all finished."

Miss Pearl twirled the chair back again, and Mona looked at her drippy reflection without seeing it.

"But, Miss Pearl, tell me about how you ran away."

"Well, finally I just couldn't stand it any more. She used to beat me up something terrible, and she kept us working all day long. She wouldn't let us go to school even. Well, one afternoon she caught me reading a book when I was supposed to be mending, so she took the book and threw it in the stove and then she whipped me good. It was just too much. I sneaked out to the barn where Perry was milking and I says to him: 'I won't stay any longer. I'm going to run away to an orphan asylum.' So Perry says: 'I'll go with you'; he was all excited. 'Not to an orphan asylum, though,' he says. 'We'll go to the city and make our fortunes.' Well, I have to laugh when I think of it." Miss Pearl was drying Mona's hair dreamily. "We didn't make our fortunes exactly but we made out all right."

"But tell me about the running away."

"Oh. Well, we got it all planned out. I had a heifer that was my very own; I'd raised her from a calf. Margaret, her name was. Perry had a sow called Greta that was *his* own. Besides that he had a good bicycle and Dad's gold watch. We never took a single thing that belonged to our stepmother. Well. So the day before we left I sneaked away and walked Margaret all the way to Verona, near five miles. I sold her, too. Gee, I felt bad but I had to do it. She was a good heifer and they paid me fifty dollars for her, and would have paid me more if I'd been grown up instead of a kid. Well, anyway, fifty dollars made me feel like I was Mrs. John D. Rockefeller."

"I should think so," said Mona. "What about Greta?"

"Oh, she was a mean sow. Big as a kitchen range and, my, was she mean. Perry couldn't have walked *her* to Verona, so he did the next best thing. He went to our neighbor, a farmer named Mr. Ruxton who knew Greta well because she'd busted loose and eaten a whole row of onions in his garden once. He knew she was a good sow and he gave Perry a fine price for her; and after Perry'd sold the watch and the bike and all we figured we were rich." Miss Pearl began combing Mona's hair. "So the next night, maybe ten o'clock, after our stepmother was asleep, we packed everything we owned (which wasn't much) into an old wicker suitcase of our father's. Perry looked at me. 'You ought to do something different with your hair,' he says. 'Why?' I says. 'Well,' he says, 'you look too much like a kid. And anyway for disguise. You ought to do something with it, put it up or something.' "

"How old were you?" asked Mona.

"Thirteen, going on fourteen, and Perry, he was nearly sixteen. Well, but I couldn't put it up because we hadn't any pins. So Perry says, 'I know! We'll cut it off.' We often kid about it now; he should've gone into the hairdressing business, I tell him, instead of me. He showed a real talent for it, I tell him. Honest, you should have seen me! He just took a pair of shears and cut off my hair like you'd cut off a bunch of grass with a sickle. Was I a sight! Perry says: 'Well, you look worse but you look older.'

"So we sneaked out of the house! The only way to get down was by the front stairs and Perry had a pair of new shoes that squealed like puppies. The suitcase thumped against the banisters and our hearts were right up where our tonsils were." Miss Pearl leaned out of the booth. "Oh, Mr. *Ed*-ward," she called, "we're ready for you."

"Please go on," begged Mona.

"Okay, honey," said Miss Pearl. "Do you want a manicure?"

"Yes, I do," said Mona recklessly. "I never had one in my life, and goodness knows when I'll ever have another chance." She shut Cuffy's disapproving face out of her mind. Just this once, she told herself.

Miss Pearl went out of the booth and reappeared with a little table on wheels. She sat down at the table, snapped on a light, and reached out for Mona's hand, which she placed on a covered cushion. Mona stared with interest at the little bottles and the instruments on the table.

"Let's see, where was I?" said Miss Pearl, taking up Mona's hand and beginning to file her nails. She was much more gentle about this, too, than Cuffy was.

"You were going downstairs," Mona reminded her.

"Yes. Well, we got downstairs all right, and we left a note for our stepmother on the mantel telling her we were never coming back. (I guess she was glad to be rid of us.) But *then* we had to walk all the way to Verona. The suitcase weighed a ton. Perry'd carry it first one hand, then the next. Then I'd carry it a little ways. Then we'd both sit down on it and rest."

Mr. Edward, flourishing a comb, made his villain's entrance into the booth. "*Now* then, little lady," he said, and began curling Mona's wet hair up into little snails like Cuffy's, and stabbing them together with hairpins.

"Go on, Miss Pearl," commanded Mona hastily, before Mr. Edward could think of any more questions.

"Finally we did get to Verona. We went to the depot there and hoped there'd be a train. My brother made me go in and buy the tickets because he figured the station agent, Mr. Kraus, wouldn't be so apt to recognize me with my hair cut and all. I had a hat on too, and tried to act like I was sixteen years old. The next train didn't come till midnight. We sat outside on one of those hard benches, and all we could hear was the crickets and tree toads in the woods across the tracks. Dip your hand, honey."

Mona dipped her fingers in a little bowl of soapy water.

"Finally the train came, and we sat up all night in the

coach. There was a baby that cried all the time, like there always is, and a fat man that snored fit to beat the band. I never heard anything like it. I guess we slept though, all right, because the next we knew it was morning and the conductor was hollering: 'G-rand Central Station!' 'Does he mean it's New York?' I says to Perry, and we asked him, and he says 'Where else?'

"Well, we went walking around the streets looking up at the high buildings till our necks ached, and that darn suitcase weighing like a grand piano. We were sort of bewildered, I guess. We'd never seen so many people in our lives and we'd never heard such noise. 'I wish I'd gone to an orphan asylum instead,' I says, just about ready to cry. But Perry got mad. 'I think it's swell,' he says. 'I'm going to live here forever.' The funny thing is that Perry's married now, and running a poultry farm in Jersey; and here I am still in the city, and crazy about it."

"Then what happened, Miss Pearl?"

"We just walked around and asked at all the places where there were signs saying 'Vacant Rooms.' But all the places were too expensive and most of the people we talked to wouldn't have taken us anyhow. We looked too young, I guess, and kind of bewildered. That night we went back to Grand Central Station and dozed sitting up in the waiting room. You can take your hand out now, dear."

"Why, Pearl, you never told me all this before," said Mr. Edward. "What have you been keeping from me?"

"Well, it's all so long ago." Miss Pearl laughed self-consciously. "Seems like a dream now. Anyway, the next day we found a boardinghouse way downtown on the East Side, and they didn't care what we looked like and it was cheap, so they took us in. We felt fine. It seemed to us like our money would last forever, and we bought some new clothes (as grown-up looking as we could get), and then spent about a week going around seeing the sights: boat rides, Statue of Liberty, the Zoo, the Aquarium, up to the top of the Empire State Building, just about everything. Dip the other hand, dear."

"It must have been fun," Mona said.

"Yes, it was fun. But then our money began getting low and we got scared. Perry looked for jobs everywhere. So did I; but it was summertime and nobody seemed to be hiring anybody, and then, like I say, we probably looked too young and green. We lived for weeks on crackers and oranges. Perry got sick too, and we didn't dare get a doctor. We were too poor, and anyway we were worried they'd find out about us and ship us home, or something. Poor Perry just had to get well by himself. My, were we scared, though!"

All through this tale Miss Pearl continued to smile happily. She looks well fed now, thank goodness, Mona thought.

"And in the end it was me who got the first job. It

was a little one-horse beauty parlor up in the Bronx (naturally I let them think I was a lot older than I was). They needed a girl to sweep and clean up, and hold pins; things like that. That's how I got interested in the business. Then Perry he got a job as an office boy. Everything was okay after that. It seemed like I spent half my life in the subway (and at first it made me carsick every time). At night my feet nearly killed me. Perry had a hard time too; everybody kidded him all the time because he was green. But none of those things mattered. We were just kids, we had our health, and we'd got away from something we hated; we were earning our own livings decently, and gee, we felt like a couple of Christopher Columbuses or something. It seemed to us like nobody'd ever done such a thing before!"

"Quite a little story, Pearl," said Mr. Edward, tying a net over Mona's snailed-up hair. "Quite a little story, isn't it, Lorna? What they call a human interest story."

"Well, I think it's wonderful!" said Mona fervently. "The most adventurous thing I ever did was to come here and get my hair cut. I think it's a wonderful story."

Mr. Edward wheeled in one of the bell-shaped driers that Mona had noticed in the other room. It grew on a tall stem like a gigantic lily and had a long tendril of wire. Mr. Edward adjusted the bell over Mona's head, snapped a switch and released a small warm tempest that swarmed suddenly through her hair, and filled her ears with a gentle roaring.

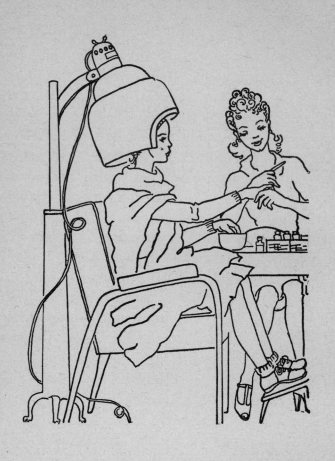

Miss Pearl leaned forward asking a question that Mona couldn't hear. She supposed it was something about whether or not she was comfortable and nodded her head absently. There she sat in her small windy cave staring at Miss Pearl's long eyelashes against her cheek, and the contented smile that curved her lips. Her face looked pretty and a little bit foolish; and yet she was brave and strong and adventurous, and had worked hard since she was a little child. Sometimes people are not the way they look, thought Mona. It was a great surprise.

She was so absorbed in these reflections that it came as a frightful shock when Miss Pearl gave her back one of her hands to look at. All five nails had been painted red as blood! Mona was horrified and fascinated at the same time. Cuffy would faint dead away if she ever saw them, but they were so beautiful! Like little red shells, or curved rubies, or even drops of sealing wax, but nothing at all like fingernails. After all, I can take it off when I get home, Mona told herself. I'll just keep them this way till I get back and look at them once in a while.

"They're perfect," she said, and Miss Pearl's smile was more pleased than ever as she began on the other hand. By and by, when Mona's hair was cooked enough she reached over and switched off the tempest. In the sudden clear stillness Mona could hear the lady in booth twelve telling some one about how she'd eaten something that disagreed with her.

"Well, my dear, I was in agony!" she was saying.

"Absolute agony. And *hives!* Well, I had hives the size of fifty-cent pieces all over me. I kept wondering could it have been the lobster? But my husband, Mr. Elenbogen, said, 'Why, Grace, you *know* lobsters never affect you.' Then I wondered maybe it was that rich dessert. That's what I think it must have been, that rich dessert."

"Maybe it was the combination," observed a patient voice.

"No, I think it was the dessert. You know I almost *never* eat dessert," said the woman as if this were a fact of the most vital interest.

"There we are, honey," Miss Pearl said, wheeling away the drier, and beginning to take the hairpins out.

"I feel like a baked potato," Mona remarked, "and I look a lot like one too."

"Now you just wait, honey," Miss Pearl told her. "You just wait till we get rid of these old pins and Mr. Edward combs you out. You won't *know* yourself."

And it was true. Ten minutes later, after Mr. Edward had combed and brushed and snipped and fussed over her hair, Mona did not know herself. Great curls and puffs and ringlets frothed above her shoulders and on her forehead. The result exceeded her wildest expectations. She was awed by the beauty of it. Why, I could go into the movies this minute, she thought; only what would Cuffy say?

"Honey, you're a picture!" exclaimed Miss Pearl,

clasping her hands in admiration. "I bet you somebody's going to cause quite a sensation when she goes home. I bet her daddy won't know her; he'll be tickled to death!"

Mona had a small pang of misgiving when she thought of Father. Tickled to death wasn't exactly what she expected him to be. But maybe he'd like it when he got used to it.

"Yes, indeed, little lady," Mr. Edward was saying. "You are definitely the subdeb type. Definitely. Just remember I told you so, Myra."

Mona wasn't exactly sure of what he meant by "subdeb type," but she supposed it was a compliment, so she said "thank you" and shook hands with both him and Miss Pearl.

Even the Tang goddess at the desk cracked her mask with a smile.

"You look real cute, dear," she said. "That'll be a dollar fifty."

Well, that took the last penny in Mona's purse, and it was a long way home, but never mind.

All over the city lights were coming on in the purple-blue dusk. The street lights looked delicate and frail, as though they might suddenly float away from their lamp-posts like balloons. Long twirling ribbons of light, red, green, violet, were festooned about the doorways of drugstores and restaurants—and the famous electric signs of Broadway had come to life with glittering fish, dancing figures, and leaping fountains, all flashing like fire. Everything was beautiful. Up in the deepening sky above the city the first stars appeared white and rare as diamonds.

The curls bounced on Mona's shoulders. They blew softly, silkily against her cheek; and inside her gloves she could feel the ten red finger nails sparkling lightheartedly. It was a long walk home but Mona was carried swiftly on a tide of joy. It's something to discover that you're going to grow up beautiful instead of ugly.

The first person she saw when she got home was Willy Sloper shambling through the front hall on his way to Father's study. Something was probably wrong with the furnace again.

"Hello, miss," he said. "You lookin' for someone? Why—why, Mona! What you been and done to yourself?"

"Don't you like it, Willy?"

"I dunno, Mona. Maybe I do. I ain't sure. I kinda liked them plats of yours."

Oh, well, Willy doesn't know anything, Mona told herself. All the same she tiptoed up the stairs to the top floor. It was Randy's week to take care of the Office and Mona was fairly sure of finding her alone.

She was right. Music was pouring out of the radio and Randy was performing the role of Cinderella in an imaginary ballet. She went leaping and pirouetting around the room flapping the dustcloth along the shelves. Pleasure combined with work whenever possible, was Randy's idea. Mona pulled off her hat. "Look at me!" she ordered.

Randy paused in the middle of an arabesque.

"Good night! Why, Jiminy Crickets! Why, gee whiz! Why, Mona! You look wonderful but how did you ever dare? What will Father say? What will Cuffy say?"

"Well, it's too late for anybody to say anything," Mona retorted. She was feeling a little scared but it wouldn't do to let Randy know it.

"Look," she said, pulling something out of her pocket. It was the heavy shining bundle of shorn hair. "Marilyn and all the other dolls can have new wigs, and we'll save what's left over to make mustaches for plays!"

Randy's delight was the last pleasant thing about Mona's afternoon: after that everything was horrible. Absolutely horrible. Father could hardly believe that she had done such a thing without consulting him. Cuffy was frankly disgusted, and Rush said, "Jeepers! You look just like everybody. Any of those dumb high school girls that walk along the street screaming and laughing and bumping into people. Why couldn't you have waited a while?"

Oliver was the only one who reacted favorably. He said that she looked exactly like the Blue Fairy in *Pinocchio*, and Mona gave him a grateful hug.

And then the nail polish wouldn't come off. No matter how she scrubbed with soap and water the ten red nails continued to glitter unscathed. She tried cold cream, and cleaning fluid, even peroxide. By the time Cuffy blew the two blasts on the police whistle which meant dinner Mona was in a panic. She couldn't eat dinner with her gloves on, and she was too hungry to go without it. She went reluctantly down the stairs with red cheeks and her hands in her pockets.

It was a very difficult meal. Everyone kept looking at her as if she were a stranger; but the red fingernails were what bothered her the most. The left hand could be kept hidden under the napkin in her lap, but the right hand was another matter. She tried holding her fork with all the fingers curved under, which is almost impossible to do, and prayed that nobody would notice. But naturally the prayer was not worthy of an answer.

"Mona!" said Father suddenly. "What on earth is the matter with your hand, have you hurt it? Open it out and let me see."

Mona opened her hand. The five red nails were bright as stop lights and she wished that she knew how to faint at will.

"Good Lord!" said Father, and choked on his coffee.

Rush gave a long, rude whistle. "Vanity," he said pompously, "thy name sure is woman!"

Randy just looked shocked and kept on eating, and Cuffy made a snapping noise with her tongue against her teeth and shook her head as if she couldn't believe her eyes.

"What in heaven's name has got into you, Mona?"

inquired Father, red-faced from choking. "I never thought you were silly or vain. When you're eighteen years old if you want to go in for that sort of thing it will be all right, I suppose. But not now. There's no way we can bring your braids back, but at least we don't have to put up with those talons. I want you to take that red business off your nails immediately after dinner."

"It won't come off," said Mona miserably. "I tried. It has to wear off."

"I'll get it off all right," said Cuffy grimly. "There's plenty of things I can try: gasoline, or sandpaper, or shellac. But I'll get it off!"

Mona bent over her plate. There was such a lump in her throat that she could hardly swallow, and the knives and forks and glasses swam to and fro like fish.

"When are you going to start putting stuff on your face, Mona?" inquired Rush virtuously. "When are you going to start wearing a ring in your nose?"

"Oh, Rush, I hate you!" cried Mona. And she sprang up from the table and fled from the room with a loud undignified sob that came out of her like a hiccup.

Up the stairs she ran blindly. Up to the Office with the door banged behind her, and then face down in the dark on the humpy old couch which received her tenderly. She felt hurt and angry and silly and ashamed all at the same time. There was no comfort anywhere; nothing but the harsh fabric under her cheek that smelled of age and dust.

Out of doors people were walking in the street; Mona could hear their footsteps ringing on the pavement far below. Automobiles containing people whose families loved them hooted by in the winter night. I wish I could run away like Miss Pearl, Mona thought to herself. She would simply disappear, and then, years later, when she came back to New York as a famous actress, they would all (Cuffy and everyone) come to her begging forgiveness. And she would be very sweet to them.

Cuffy came into the Office and creaked down on the sofa beside her.

"Go away!" said Mona.

"No, I won't," retorted Cuffy. "You sit up like you had some spine to you."

Mona sat up.

"There's nothing to be breaking your heart about, neither. Everybody does fool things once in a while; I shouldn't be surprised if it was good for 'em." Cuffy was stroking Mona's forehead. Her hand was rough from hard work, and yet it was soft at the same time. Mona sniffled and gulped.

Above the distant noises of the city another sound, high up, purred across the night.

"Listen!" said Cuffy. "Get up, child, and come to the window. Look out."

Every house in the street was bright with windows. A vast luminous glow rose upward from the city, and high overhead against the stars there was a green star that traveled steadily.

"Look up at that," commanded Cuffy. "Nobody, hardly, looks up any more. We hear airplanes without listening to 'em. We aren't scared of them because they're as much a part of the way we get to places as busses or trolleys or railway trains. They won't harm us; we don't have to be afraid they'll drop bombs on us. And now look at all them buildings lit up like birthday cakes. There'll be lights all over this city until morning. We don't have to crawl through the black, like moles. Not yet anyway. Think of Oliver fast asleep in his little bedroom downstairs, and the good comfortable bed you're going to go to sleep in soon. There's not going to be no loud noise to wake you up at midnight and send you down cellar like a scared animal. There's lots can't say the same. Right now, right this minute, hundreds of children are fast asleep in subway stations, or down in boiler rooms. Think of the good supper you didn't eat because you was too concerned about yourself. Right now there's hundreds of children—"

"Oh, Cuffy, don't!" sobbed Mona. "I feel so cheap, I feel so cheap!" The red nails burned her fingertips like coals of fire.

"Well now, well now," said Cuffy, patting her on the shoulder blades. "It's all right, my lamb. Just quit thinking you're the hub of the universe, that's all. As for the bobbed hair, I'm not sure but what I think it's a good idea; we won't go through such perdition shampooing it from now on, and the snarls will be scarcer. But them nails—! Seems to me like I read some place perfumery would take it off."

"I have some perfume, Cuffy!" cried Mona, happy to make a sacrifice. "You wait here."

In a moment she was back with "Night on the Nile," the precious bottle which had never been opened!

"My," gasped Cuffy as the top came off, "sort of blinds you, don't it?"

"I like perfume to be really strong," Mona said, sniffing rapturously. "I like it so strong that people can come into a room twenty-four hours after you've left, and know that you've been there."

"Well, this is strong all right," said Cuffy, scrubbing away. "I bet it would take the veneer right off a piana, let alone them little nails of yours."

Soon the nails were in their natural state once more, and both Cuffy and Mona were extremely highly scented.

"I feel like Lillian Russell," remarked Cuffy. "All I need is a picture hat and diamond bracelets right up to my elbow."

Mona went down to the study to say good night to Father. The desk was littered with papers and books, and above the confusion stood the little Tang goddess looking serenely into space.

Mona held out her hands with their plain unvarnished nails.

"That's better," said Father, and took one of the hands in his. He sniffed inquiringly.

"We had to use perfume to get it off," Mona explained hastily. "It wasn't because of vanity this time."

Father laughed. "You know, Mona," he said, "maybe I'll get used to that hair of yours when it quiets down a little. Maybe I'll even like it. I suppose parents are always startled when they see their children showing signs of growing up for the first time."

Upstairs Randy was already in bed. She watched Mona getting undressed.

"You look like a movie star, Mona," she said. "I feel as if I had Deanna Durbin, or somebody, for a roommate."

"Never mind, Randy," Mona reassured her as she went to open the window. "In a day or two all the curls will be gone and I won't look that way any more. Anyway not for years and years and years."

The black night against the window made a mirror. Mona saw herself in it: long white nightgown and floating fluffy hair. It reminded her of something. She lifted an arm in front of her and let it drop hopelessly. Then she began to speak in a low, dramatic voice.

"Thou know'st the mask of night is on my face,
    Else would a maiden blush bepaint my cheek
    For that which thou hast heard me speak to-night.

Fain would I dwell on form, fain, fain deny . . ."

"Oh, Mona, honestly!" groaned Randy. "You can be Juliet tomorrow morning. You always start being Juliet the minute you put on your nightgown. You ought to wear pajamas like me. Come on to bed. I'm sleepy."

"Okay, okay," Mona said. She opened the window wide and in rushed the wild winter night and knocked over a signed photograph of Jane Cowl.

Mona switched off the light, leaped into bed, and burrowed under the covers. In a few minutes she was warm and cozy. The shade flapped against the window as it always did, and far overhead tracing its lonely path across the dark she heard the hum of the airplane. She was safe in her bed, the house enclosed her in a shell of warm security and all about, on every side, were the members of her own family who loved and understood her so well. She felt calm and happy.

"Good night, Mona," said Randy's drowsy voice across the room.

"Good night, Ran darling," Mona said. And five minutes later she was deep asleep.

AFTER a while, very slowly, it began to be spring. There were rust-colored buds on the ailanthus trees, and one day Mona heard a blue jay in the backyard sounding countryfied and out of place. Pretty soon it would be time to go to the valley; back to the rambling old wooden house that the Melendys rented every summer. Mona was homesick thinking about it, and got all her summer clothes out of their boxes to see if she had outgrown them (which she had, and Randy was glad because now they would descend to her) and forgot to put them away again until Cuffy got after her. Rush took his baseball bat to school, and Randy wrote a poem. Oliver spent hours in the back yard digging fortifications in the mud. The seats and knees of his overalls were a constant source of despair for Cuffy.

The Independent Saturday Afternoon Adventure Club had so far been entirely successful. Randy had spent her second Saturday at the Ballet Theatre and was now able to walk on her toes quite easily, and had made a ballet skirt out of five pairs of muslin curtains that couldn't be darned any more. Rush had gone to hear Rudolf Serkin play the piano, and had been practicing furiously ever since in the hours that were not occupied by school or baseball. Mona had seen Katharine Cornell in a play and was very hard to live with as a result. She now moved queenlike and distant through a world of her own.

But this particular Saturday was Oliver's, and they had agreed to stay home. Not that he could go out by himself, of course, as they could; but in order to make him feel like a proper member of the I.S.A.A.C., they respected his Saturday and stayed at home. Also, besides giving him back the three dimes he had lent them, each added a dime of his own. "That'll be almost half what we have to spend on our Saturdays, and it will look like a million dollars to him," Rush said; it was his idea.

The day passed pleasantly enough. There was lemon pie for dessert at lunch, and afterwards Rush and Randy gave Isaac a bath in the basement washtub. He was philosophical about this ordeal by now and stood passive, though loathing every minute of it. When he was dry, they took him for a walk to show him off. Mona didn't want to go because she had borrowed some of Cuffy's big steel hairpins and was doing her hair in a pompadour just for an experiment.

The walk was a great success, and so was Isaac. People stopped them frequently to admire and pat him; and every time they asked what kind of dog he was, Rush gave them a different answer in a polite, serious voice. A Bronx beagle, he might say, or a Central Park setter, or an Interborough Rapid Transit retriever. Randy almost died.

When they came back to their own block, they could see Mona hanging out of the second-story window of their house.

"Where's Oliver?" she called, when they drew near.

Rush and Randy looked at her blankly.

"I don't know. Where is he?" shouted Rush.

"Isn't he home?" cried Randy.

"We can't find him any place," answered Mona, withdrawing her head and closing the window with a bang.

They ran up the steps and into the house. Cuffy looked pale and distracted. "Rush, you go down the street to the Potters' and see if by any chance he's gone to play with Petey, though goodness knows he's never done such a thing before. Randy, you run round the block. Maybe he's trying out his roller skates again."

"Maybe he's just hiding," suggested Randy.

"His coat and cap are gone," Mona told her. "And anyway I've looked everywhere. In all the closets and underneath the beds. Even in the trunks in the basement."

"Where's Father?"

"Gone to Philadelphia to lecture. He won't be back

till five and we don't know where to get him. Hurry up,
Randy, run along."

At that moment the object of all this concern was
seated comfortably at Madison Square Garden. His
knees were crossed, he was leaning back with a bottle
of pop in one hand, and watching a lady in spangles
hanging by her teeth to a rope fifty feet above the
ground.

It had all been very simple, but it was also a well-
thought-out campaign. Four weeks ago Oliver had received seven dimes which he had prudently concealed
in one of his last summer's sandals. Today he had
received seven more, which together with the sandal
money made fourteen dimes. Untold wealth, but he did
not let it go to his head. Everything proceeded according
to plan.

Today when he was supposed to be resting he had
got up, put on his coat and cap, and walked, faintly
jingling, right out of the house. There was no trouble
of any kind. When he got to Fifth Avenue he went up
to a policeman and said, "Where is the circus, please?"

And the policeman said, "Madison Square Garden.
Aren't you kinda young to be out alone?"

Oliver simply said, "No, I don't think so," and went
his way. When he came to another policeman some
blocks farther on he went up to him and said, "Where is
Madison Square Garden, please?"

"Going to the circus, eh?" said the policeman. "It's at Fiftieth Street and Eighth Avenue. You all alone?"

Oliver simply said, "Yes, I am," and proceeded on his way, leaving the policeman with his hands full of traffic.

At Fiftieth Street he went up to another policeman and said, "Which way is Eighth Avenue, please?"

"That way," said the policeman, jerking a white cotton thumb westward. " 'Bout three blocks over. Ain't nobody with you?"

Oliver simply said, "No, nobody," and crossed the street with the red light.

It was easy when he got there too. He just stood in a long line of grownups and children and held tight to his dimes and listened to what the people in front of him said when they got to the window. So when he got there he was able to say, "One, please. The kind that costs one dollar," and count out ten dimes slowly and carefully. The man behind the window had to peer down in order to see him at all. Then holding his ticket tightly he followed close behind a large family and tried hard to look like one of them.

"Like to hold your own ticket, eh, sonny?" said the ticket man.

"Yes, I do," replied Oliver, and entered the magic portals. It was wonderful. It smelled of elephants the minute you got in, even before you came to the real circus part. Breathing the smell deeply, Oliver climbed some steps that a uniformed man told him to, and then walked along a corridor that another uniformed man told him to. He thought he heard a lion roar some place, and his feet crunched on peanut shells. It was very exciting. Finally he came to the right door, entered it, and found himself in another world. It was a vast world, carpeted with blue sawdust and walled with thousands of faces. A complicated web of cables and rope ladders and nets rose from the huge arena to misty regions high overhead. On the blue sawdust at the bottom there were three large caged rings, and in each of these rings the most extraordinary things were happening.

"This way, Bud," said the usher, steering the bedazzled Oliver to a seat. Oliver sat down without knowing that he did so. After a long time he removed his coat and cap blindly, never taking his eyes off the ring nearest him. In it three lions, two bears, and a black leopard were climbing ladders, while on high gold stools seven other lions sat and snarled and batted with their paws at their trainer who was the bravest man in the world and wore a red coat. He could make those animals do anything. Before he was through, one of the bears was pushing the other in a huge baby carriage while all the lions, on a bridge overhead, sat up on their hind legs and begged. Oliver sighed deeply: it was almost too much. His only regret was that he was too busy watching his ring to pay attention to the others. The air rang with the crack of whips and the sharp commands of the trainers.

As the cages were dismantled and the animals taken away, Oliver began to notice the men who were going up and down the aisles selling things: jeweled canes, and clown hats, and things to eat. They called their wares hoarsely like a lot of crows. "Hot dogs, hot dogs!" cried one, and "Getcha roasted peanuts here," cried another, and "Icecole pop," still another. But the one Oliver was most interested in was the man who kept saying "Cotton candy, Cotton c-a-a-a-n-dy," as he went by with what looked like a lot of pink birds' nests on sticks. Oliver finally bought one. It was interesting; you bit into a cloud of pink spun sugar and it instantly became nothing in your mouth. He ate it lingeringly, to make it last. All the time fascinating things were going on in the huge arena before him. Clowns came out and did their stunts, a man jumped over three elephants, ladies in spangles rode standing up on the backs of broad white horses, and dozens of tiny taffy-colored ponies, with plumes on their foreheads like the frills on lamb chops, pranced delicately about the rings and performed the most astonishing tricks. Oliver bit into his pink cloud and stared dreamily.

"I want some of that candy," said a sharp little voice at his side. Oliver turned a startled glance on the occupant of the next seat. He had forgotten there was anyone else in the world besides himself and the circus people.

"Don't bother the little boy, Marleen," said the little

girl's mother in the kind of weak, uncertain way that
no self-respecting child pays any attention to.

"I *want* some," repeated Marleen through her nose.
She meant business. She was a very little girl and she
had a pointed chin, dark eyes, black curls as stiff as
cigars, a blue hair ribbon, a gold ring, and pink stuff on
her tiny fingernails. Oliver detested her. He looked
coldly away and went on eating his candy.

"Now, Marleen," said her mother.

"I want some. I *want* some of that boy's candy!"

"I'll get you some when the man comes by. Now you
be a good girl and look at the pretty horsies."

"I want some of his. You give me that candy, boy!"

Oliver swallowed the last of it at a gulp and Marleen
uttered a piercing scream of frustration. Heads in the
row turned and looked at them. "Now, Marleen, now
Marleen," said her mother helplessly. But Marleen continued to scream like a steam whistle until her mother
had consoled her by buying her a cotton-candy stick of
her own, and a fancy cane besides. Even then she stared
unblinkingly at Oliver. She could not be persuaded to
look at the arena, and after a while the consciousness
of that baleful scrutiny spoiled even Oliver's enjoyment.
He couldn't pay the proper attention to the jugglers. A
few rows away, on the aisle, he noticed a vacant seat and
after some deliberation made his way to it without a
backward glance at Marleen.

After this unpleasant episode the performance progressed blissfully without a flaw. The procession was magnificent beyond description; from zebra-drawn coaches to elephants wearing tasseled capes and jeweled howdahs. Oliver watched it raptly while eating a hot dog with mustard. He surveyed the acrobats (whose muscles seemed to stretch like garters) while eating another hot dog, this time with sauerkraut. It was forbidden Paradise. Cuffy didn't believe in hot dogs or mustard or sauerkraut, but Oliver believed in them all. By the time the aerial artists had come along he was quenching a violent thirst with a bottle of pop. (It was at this moment that his entire family was in an uproar about his disappearance.) The act was so exciting that he couldn't finish the pop till it was over, because it made his stomach feel so queer when one of the glittering creatures high overhead leaped from her fragile swing and arched through the air like a bird to the next glittering creature. The climax came when one of the creatures stood on her head on a trapeze without holding on and swung to and fro, shimmering like a dragonfly, far above the arena. It was breath-taking. Oliver felt so weak after watching her that he quickly finished his pop and purchased a bag of peanuts to fortify himself.

What a circus it was! One continual blaze of glory from beginning to end; from the flashing, bounding acrobats to the trained seals clapping their flippers; from the daring tightrope walkers to the fat clown who kept finding live ducklings in his pockets. Oliver did not want to believe it was over and sat for quite a while with people climbing over him and pushing past him, in the hope that they were all mistaken and something new was about to begin in the arena.

"Whatcha waitin' for, Bud?" said the usher, coming up to him. "Don'tcha know you'll get swept up with the trash and fed to the elephants if you wait too long?"

Probably he doesn't mean it, Oliver thought, but he got up hastily. At first he couldn't find his coat or cap, but then he remembered he had left them in the seat from which Marleen had driven him. There they still were luckily, though littered with peanut shells and a piece of chewed chewing gum, doubtless the work of the vindictive Marleen. Oliver cleaned them off as well as he could, put them on, and after quite a lot of blundering about in the wrong direction (owing to the fact that he didn't understand the meaning of the word "exit") he found himself out on the street. Already it was dusk, and he began to hurry. For the first time the probable consequences of his adventure began to trouble him. It made him especially uncomfortable to think of Cuffy, for some reason.

And now the streets kept turning out the wrong way, and he found himself on Tenth Avenue instead of Fifth. The place looked strange; full of high, dark buildings, and big noisy boys who went bowling by him on roller skates, and shouted at him hoarsely to get out of the way. As if that weren't enough, he began to have a

terrible stomach-ache. Though he was a calm and re-
sourceful person, Oliver was only six years old after all.
So the next move seemed to be to cry. He stumbled and
banged along the street, sobbing quietly and wiping his
nose on his sleeve, wishing with all his heart that he was
at home with Cuffy, and that he had never heard of hot
dogs or cotton candy. Dimly he was aware of a clopping
of hoofs on pavement but he was too miserable to look
up until he heard a voice say:

"Whatsa matter, sonny?"

Oliver saw a big square policeman seated on a big
square horse, magnificent as anything at the circus. All
his buttons and two gold teeth glittered richly in the
light of the street lamp.

"What's eatin' you?" repeated the policeman kindly.

"I'm lost!" wept Oliver, "And I'm sick at my stomach,
and I want to go *home!*"

"What's your name?"

"Oliver M-Melendy."

"Know where you live?"

Oliver told him.

"Okay. You quit crying now," said the policeman.
"You and me will take a little ride to your house. Think
ya can hold out?"

"I guess so," replied Oliver dubiously. His stomach
felt awfully unreliable. The policeman got off his horse
and hoisted Oliver up on it as if he had been a kitten.
Then he got on himself, behind Oliver, clucked at the

horse and away they went. Oliver thought gloomily that
it was probably the only time in his whole life that he
was ever going to ride with a mounted policeman and he
felt so sick he couldn't appreciate it.

"I guess I'm going to get a scolding when I go home,"
Oliver told the policeman. "Maybe I'll get a spanking
too." All the shine was gone off the day.

"Why, what did you do?"

"Will you promise not to arrest me?" said Oliver
cautiously.

"I doubt if it will be necessary," said the policeman,
so Oliver told him.

"Well, I'll let your family take care of the penalty,"
the policeman decided. "It's a very serious offense all
right, but it seems to me you've been punished almost
enough as it is."

The traffic cop at Fifth Avenue looked at the
mounted policeman and Oliver and said, "You've run in
another big-time gang leader, I see."

"You'd be surprised," replied Oliver's policeman, and
gave Oliver a pat on the shoulder.

At the Melendy house all was confusion. Randy was
in tears. Father (who had returned from Philadelphia)
and Rush were still out searching, and Cuffy was saying
into the telephone, "Six years old, He has blue eyes,
blond hair, and he weighs—" when the doorbell rang,
and she dropped the receiver.

"Oh, Oliver darling, where were you?" cried Mona's

voice, and Cuffy arrived to see her on her knees beside Oliver, who looked smaller and paler than ever before. Behind him stood the largest, most solid policeman she had ever seen in her life.

Aching with relief, Cuffy hugged Oliver, then she looked up at the policeman and said, "That's the quickest response I ever got from anything. I hadn't no more than just finished describing him to the police this minute—"

"The police force is never at a loss, ma'am," replied the officer with a wink.

Cuffy held Oliver away from her:

"Where in the world have you been?"

"To the circus," replied Oliver wanly.

"To the circus! Alone?" Cuffy was horrified.

"I wouldn't be too hard on him, ma'am," advised the officer.

"Go ahead and spank me if you want to," Oliver said, and was sick on the doormat.

Long, long afterwards, when all the thunder and lightning in his stomach had subsided, and the danger of a spanking was past, Oliver lay in his small bed with his hand in Father's.

"Why did you go without telling us, though?" asked Father. "You could have gone to the circus. Rush or Cuffy would have been glad to take you. I would have taken you myself if I could have stolen the time."

Oliver sighed. "I did ask Cuffy about it once, but she

said oh no there's too much measles around. And everybody else was going out alone on their Saturdays, so I just thought I'd go alone too. I did want to see the circus so badly."

"Didn't you know we'd worry?"

"I guess I didn't think about it till afterwards," Oliver admitted.

"Well, you'll never give us a scare like that again, will you?"

"No, I never will, if I can help it," promised Oliver.

"All right then. That's that. Now suppose you tell me what you liked best at the circus."

"Oh, everything was wonderful. I liked the man on the one-wheel bicycle, and the elephants, and that automobile with all the clowns and the donkey in it, and the lady who stood on her head on the swing, and I liked all the things I was eating, while I was eating them. But the thing I liked *best* of all wasn't in the circus."

"What was that?" said Father.

"It was when the policeman brought me home on the horse," replied Oliver.

For now, no longer overshadowed by stomach-aches or unhappy apprehensions, the memory of that ride had become a radiant thing. He remembered the horse's two pointed ears that could move independently of each other, and its brawny, arching neck with the tidy black mane; and its strong, healthy smell. It was sort of like riding on a boat, only better because it felt alive, and you were higher up. And behind, immense and gorgeous in his uniform, rode the officer of the law who had befriended him. Oliver remembered how he held the reins in white gloved hands the size of baseball mitts. The splendor of that ride would never die.

A FTER Oliver's Saturday the senior members of the I.S.A.A.C. went to Father in a body and Randy (because she was president) was spokesman. Her speech was short and to the point.

"We've decided this business of going off by ourselves isn't such a good idea after all. We've decided to all do something together every Saturday instead, so Oliver can do it too."

"A sound idea," Father approved. "I was going to suggest it myself, but I much prefer having it come from you."

So that was all right. The thing was deciding on something they all wanted to do that could be done within the limits of a dollar and sixty cents.

"How about the Empire State Building?" suggested Rush.

"Heights make my stomach feel queer," Mona objected. "And besides it costs too much."

"How about the Statue of Liberty?" said Randy.

"Heights make my stomach feel queer," repeated Mona patiently.

"Let's go up in an airplane!" cried Oliver excitedly. Rush just looked at him.

"For a dollar and sixty cents?" he said.

"And besides *heights make my stomach feel queer!*" insisted Mona in exasperation.

"Well, they say you don't notice it so much in a plane, but anyway it's out of the question," Randy said. "I know what. Let's take our lunch in a basket and have a picnic in Central Park. We can plan a what-do-you-call-it for next Saturday and the ones after it."

"A campaign," said Rush. He sat down on the piano bench and improvised a march.

"Well, it's rather cold," murmured Mona doubtfully. "Willy's even got the furnace going."

"But it's May," Randy said firmly. "It *ought* to be warm. And anyway who minds a little cold? We can take extra sweaters, and have hot cocoa in the thermos bottle."

At last it was agreed upon. Cuffy told them just what they could take from the icebox and Rush adroitly managed to smuggle half an apple pie and a jar of pickled onions besides.

"You girls and Oliver will have to carry the things," he told them blandly. "I'll meet you at the zoo entrance at half past twelve."

"Why? Why can't you come with us?" asked Mona, a little resentfully.

"They don't allow dogs on the bus," explained Rush. "And we can't go without Isaac."

Naturally they couldn't. Mona made no further objections.

On their way out they met Willy Sloper wandering forlornly through the kitchen hall.

"Hello, kids," whispered Willy huskily.

"Why aren't you talking out loud, Willy?" questioned Randy, whispering too. "What's the secret?"

"Laryngitis," whispered Willy, thumping his collarbone. "Can't talk. Haven't feltsa foolish sincema voice changed."

"You go see Cuffy," ordered Mona firmly. "She can fix anything like that. She's wonderful at curing people."

"Merely a matter of castor oil, old man," said Rush heartily, or heartlessly, depending on how you looked at it.

"And gargling and gargling and gargling," said Mona.

"And mustard plasters that burn like bonfires," contributed Randy.

"Mustard plasters! Gargling! Castor oil!" cried Oliver, squeaking swiftly down the banisters. "I'm certainly glad it's not me," he said as he banged against the newel post at the bottom and dismounted.

"I wish it wasn't me neither," croaked Willy gloomily,

departing in search of Cuffy. "Well, g'bye, kids. You have yourselves a good time."

"Oh, Willy, I wish you were coming too," said Randy sorrowfully. "But it wouldn't be good for your laryngitis."

"Rush, you hurry and go on ahead with Isaac or we'll be there hours ahead of you," directed Mona. But as it turned out he was only twenty minutes late, and they had a wonderful time watching the seals until he came.

"Let's find a picnic place right away," Randy suggested. "I don't know why it is, but whenever I have a picnic basket with me I can hardly wait to begin eating."

After a while they found a place; quite near the lake in a hollow between some rocks where it wasn't so cold. Now and then the sun looked almost as though it were going to come out, but it never did quite. The Melendys didn't mind. The hot cocoa was exactly right and Mona had created some unusual sandwiches composed of peanut butter, mayonnaise, brown sugar, grape jelly, and lettuce all at once between enormous slabs of bread.

"Big as monuments," Rush commented approvingly. "I like sandwiches to be so thick you have to open your mouth like a yawn to take a bite. Then you know you've really got something."

"What's in them, anyway?" asked Randy.

Mona's acting look came over her face.

'Eye of newt,' " she replied dreamily. " 'And toe
of frog,
Wool of bat, and tongue of dog,
Adder's fork, and blind-worm's sting.
Lizard's leg, and—' "

"Mainly peanut butter, I should guess," said Rush
practically. "But good, anyway."

Isaac kept sitting up on his hind legs and crooning
pathetically. They all gave him pieces of this and that.
"He's going to be a very fat, unsightly dog if we don't
look out," Rush said, tossing him a pickle, which he ate.
He ate anything.

"Thou cream-faced loon!" said Mona. "You'll make
him sick."

"Cream-faced—*what* did you call me?" demanded
Rush indignantly.

"It's Shakespeare," Mona explained hastily. "*Macbeth*. Look it up if you don't believe me. I always sort
of liked the way it sounded. I suppose the witch poem
must have made me think of it."

"Oh, well, if it's Shakespeare I suppose it's all right.
I thought it was something you made up yourself. You'll
have to be a very good actress when you grow up to
justify all the Shakespeare we've had to listen to."

"You'll have to be a very good pianist," retorted
Mona, "to justify the nine hundred and sixty-seven times
we've had to listen to you plow through the Revolutionary Etude."

"And I'll have to be a very good dancer," Randy said peaceably, "to justify all the pounding and leaping I've done all my life."

"When I grow up," Oliver interjected suddenly, "I'm not going to be a train engineer after all."

"What are you going to be, darling?" Mona asked.

"A policeman on a horse," replied Oliver raptly, reaching for a piece of pie.

When they had eaten all they could, and the leftovers were put back in the basket till they could find a wastepaper receptacle, they began to wonder what they should do next. Randy wanted to go back to the zoo, but that was out of the question because Isaac was with them and dogs were not allowed. Mona would have liked to feed the leftover crusts to the ducks in the bird sanctuary, but it was Oliver who decided the question. He wanted to go out on the lake in a rowboat; and that seemed a good idea to everyone, even though the day was raw and grey. Rush wasn't sure whether dogs were allowed or not, so they did Isaac up in a sweater just to be on the safe side and Mona carried him under her arm like a bundle. The boat wasn't expensive, thank goodness; forty-five cents for all of them, and they would have something left over for next time. They fitted into the boat neatly: Rush at the oars, Randy and Isaac in the bow, Mona and Oliver in the stern. Rush rowed very well. The water was a dark, thick green that looked almost solid until Rush cut into it with the oars and it

broke into curling, wavering patterns of light and dark, speckled with bubbles. There was only one other boat out today. A stout elderly man was rowing at terrific speed. His face was red and he was frowning.

"I bet he does it because he thinks the exercise will make him smaller around the middle," whispered Mona. "He looks as if it were medicine instead of fun."

Randy leaned far out over the bow and stared down at her own reflected face: dark lips and eyes, wild, curling hair. It looked different and new like the face of a stranger, but it didn't interest her for long. Deep down through the face she could see things: a trailing weed, something round and white (was it a shell?), glimpsed for a second and then lost; a shimmer of metal that could have been a silver bracelet, or a dagger, or an old tin can. Probably an old tin can.

"I like water," Randy said.

"I like milk," said Oliver.

"I don't mean to drink. I mean to look at or play with or get into. Dark-green water in lakes like this, and salt water with big waves and a fishy smell; and water coming loud over a dam, and water in brooks all full of caddis houses and green moss. And water in swamps with cattails growing out of it. And yellow mudpuddle water that you can wade in, with the mud as soft as butter between your toes."

"And water in the bathtub with Cuffy scrubbing the skin off you," added Rush. "And water on the brain like I think you've got. Ah, yes, my friends. Water is a wonderful thing."

"Well, I like milk," said Oliver.

"Oh, look!" cried Randy excitedly. "A big fish! I swear I saw a big fish." She stood up, leaning far out.

"Where, where?" demanded Oliver, leaping to his feet. The boat lurched, Isaac barked, and Randy fell overboard with a loud splash.

"Oh, boy!" murmured Rush in an awed voice. "Now what will Cuffy say!"

Randy's startled face reappeared almost instantly; her curls plastered flat to her head. "Gee whiz!" she gasped breathlessly, swimming to the boat. "Is it ever cold!"

"Still crazy about water?" asked Rush, reaching out an oar for her to catch.

"I guess so," replied Randy doubtfully, grabbing it. "But it's not so easy to swim in shoes and two sweaters and all your other clothes besides."

Rush and Mona pulled her into the boat at the risk of capsizing it. Oliver bounced excitedly up and down on the stern seat, Isaac barked, the picnic basket fell over and disgorged cups, spoons, papers and oranges all over the floor of the boat. It was a scene of the wildest confusion. By the time they had Randy aboard they were all more wet than dry, and she was as drenched as anyone can ever be without being drowned. Rush pulled off his jacket gallantly and wrapped it around her. Mona gave her her top sweater and tried to dry her hair with a paper napkin.

"We'd better beat it," said Rush, rowing furiously toward the pier.

The odd thing was that the man in charge of the boats seemed more annoyed than sympathetic about the episode, and remarked several times that this here was not no swimmin' pool like some dumb kids seemed to think.

"Now we'll have to take a taxi," said Mona in resignation. "There goes the surplus."

"The what?" asked Randy breathlessly. They were all dogtrotting to the nearest exit from the park, with Oliver some yards behind bleating "Wait for me!"

"The I.S.A.A.C. money for today she means," Rush replied jerkily. "But it doesn't matter at all."

"It can't be helped anyway," said Mona.

"I'm sorry," gasped Randy, thudding moistly along. "Maybe it wasn't a fish, even."

"Don't you worry, Ran. It was sort of an adventure, after all," Mona comforted her. "I never heard of anyone falling overboard in Central Park before."

"Wait for me-e-e!" wailed Oliver, far behind.

Finally they reached the gate and found a taxi. The driver was a very nice man named Yasha Minczkotski who roared with laughter when they explained what had happened. He seemed to share Mona's view.

"You fell outa boat in Centra Park? In Centra Park? Outa *boat?* Wait'll I tell my kid."

"How old is your kid?" asked Mona politely.

"Nine year," replied Mr. Minczkotski.

"B-boy or g-girl?" asked Randy, her teeth chattering.

"Boy. Crazy over boats. Wait'll I tell um."

By some miraculous stroke of luck Cuffy was out when they got home. Father was in New Haven, speaking at a banquet, and was not expected back till after midnight.

"Nobody'll ever need to know," said Randy in relief. "I won't have to take medicine or go to bed with a hot-water bag or anything."

"You'll have to take your shoes and socks off here in the hall. I'll get a towel. Otherwise you'd leave wet footprints all over the stair carpet and Cuffy'd be bound to find out," said Mona sensibly.

"What about all these wet clothes though?" Randy trudged barefoot and shivering up the stairs. "The wettest thing in the world to wear is a wet sweater!"

"Take them all off and give them to me. I'll hang them up in the furnace room," said Mona. "Willy won't tell if we ask him not to. And you'd better take a good hot bath, Ran."

When Cuffy returned at four o'clock she found the Melendy children up in the Office, peacefully employed. Rush was playing the Golliwog's Cakewalk; Randy was practicing standing on her toes, Mona was reading, and

Oliver was painting large pictures of the circus with a great deal of paint, mostly red.

"Did you have a nice time?" inquired Cuffy. "I was afraid it was going to rain. I thought to myself they'll get caught in a shower and come home soaking wet."

"No, Cuffy," Randy said. "We didn't get caught in a shower!"

Cuffy couldn't understand why they all snorted with giggles at that. She didn't see anything funny about it.

At bedtime Cuffy said, "Well, I suppose I'd better go down and put the furnace to bed too."

Mona looked up, startled. "Why? Where's Willy? Is his laryngitis worse?"

"I told him to stay home in bed a day or two. We could look out for the furnace, I told him."

"Let me do it, Cuffy," pleaded Rush. He'd had a sudden vision of all Randy's clothes drying on the basement clothesline. "I'd *like* to do it. Really I would."

"Well, all right, Rush. I don't know's there's any reason why you shouldn't."

"And every reason why I should," said Rush significantly, with a wink at Randy. Besides concealing the evidence of her mishap from Cuffy this was an excellent opportunity to get Isaac out of the basement and up to the forbidden haven of his room.

At last all the good nights had been said, all the doors closed, all the teeth brushed. The night wind sucked in the window shades and then blew them out again with a sighing sound. Sometime in the night Rush half awoke to hear a thunderous downpour of rain, and the sound of Cuffy closing windows all over the house. He just had time to get Isaac under the bed and sink into deep simulated slumber himself when Cuffy came into his room and closed the window. He could hear her clicking her tongue and muttering, "Teeming! It's simply teeming." Why do people always say it *teems* when it rains hard? Rush wondered drowsily, and went to sleep again. It was the deepest darkest sleep he had ever had. For hours there wasn't even a dream in it, and then at last there was a dream.

Far, far away a dog was barking. In his dream Rush could see it: a tiny dog sitting in a lighted doorway at the end of a long passage. Funny how clearly I can see it at this distance, thought Rush in his dream; it must be at least a mile away, and yet I can even see the little freckled places on its muzzle. "Be quiet," he said to the dog. "Be quiet, let me go in peace: I want to go away without any noise." But instead of being quiet the tiny dog suddenly expanded and grew enormous, big as a house, towering above Rush; and his barking was terrible, unbearable and overwhelming. Rush opened his eyes wearily. It took him several minutes to realize that it was Isaac who was barking.

"Isaac, Isaac, what's the matter?" Rush's words came out slowly. He felt queer: as though he were still in the dream. Isaac continued to bark. "Oh, do please shut up," begged Rush. "All I want to do is go back to sleep, and how can I if you make such a racket?" Isaac paid no attention. He ran to the closed door and back again, barking all the time in a shrill nervous way as though he were afraid. It's strange he doesn't seem to have wakened anyone, wondered Rush. I'd have thought Cuffy would be in here long before this, giving us both the dickens. His arm felt heavy as lead as he searched for the light switch. What's that funny *smell*? His heart began to beat a little faster with an unknown fear, though still heavily, laboriously, as though he were carrying a burden up a hill. His hand found the switch and the room sprang into light. Everything looked the same. The big tin alarm clock ticked loudly like his own heart, and its severe black hands both pointed to three. There was the pile of tattered scores, and the tennis racket, and the nine big airplane models, and the bookcase with all its litter of books. There were his clothes, his empty socks hanging sadly over the chair arm, and his shoes on the floor, one upright and one toppled on its side. Everything just as usual. Yet was it? There was that funny smell, there was that heavy feeling in his chest, and the way he saw everything so clear and yet so distant. There was Isaac's barking.

Rush swung his legs over the edge of the bed. When he sat up straight he felt queerer than ever. "That smell," Rush said out loud to the frenzied Isaac. "I know that smell but I can't think what it is." For some reason

he began to think of a movie he had seen several years
ago. Again he saw the hero fallen forward across the
papers on his desk. "What's the matter? Why did he
die?" He'd asked Mona, and Mona had said, "Are there
any more caramels in that bag? He's dead of coal gas.
His wife put too much coal on the fire."

Like a diver on the ocean floor Rush staggered clum-
sily to the door and pulled it open. The smell was terrible. Everything looked the same and yet he knew that
an evil power was coiling through the house like some
invisible, venomous serpent. He hurried past Father's
empty room and down the stairs, banging at Cuffy's
door, and when there was no answer he hurried in and
threw open both the windows.

"Cuffy, Cuffy!" he called urgently, shaking her plump
shoulder.

"What's the matter?" said Cuffy at last. "Why in the
world are you hollerin' so? Look out, don't knock over
my teeth." She reached down for the tumbler.

"Hurry, hurry!" cried Rush. "It's coal gas! The house
is full of it. Get Oliver awake and take him outdoors!"

"What in the world—why is Isaac barking so? *Coal
gas?*" Cuffy, awake at last, sprang out of bed in her
huge white nightgown. "Where are the girls?"

But Rush was already in their room, opening the windows and calling them. The window shades stood out
flat on the draft. Rain streamed in and the city odor

of damp and soot and wet cement was like the breath
of heaven itself.

"Mona Mona Mona!" shouted Rush. "Get up. Get
up. We're being suffocated to death!"

"Oh, I don't care, I want to sleep," begged Mona and
buried her head under her pillow. She wanted to sleep
more than she had ever wanted anything in the world;
to sink deeper and deeper into this velvety, fathomless,
dreamless sleep. "Wake up! Wake up!" bawled Rush in
a voice like iron as he pulled the pillow away. "Coal gas,
I tell you! It'll kill you! Wake up!"

Mona opened her eyes. Oh, how hard it was. How
horrible to come back again.

"My head hurts so terribly," she wailed. "Coal gas?
You mean like in that Paul Muni picture we saw?"

"That's right, that's what made me know what it
was. That and Isaac. Hurry up, Mona, put on some
shoes and a coat. You'll have to help me with Randy.
I can't get her to wake up."

Mona was ready in an instant. She bundled Randy
into a coat and socks; shoes took too long.

"Shake her some more, Rush." Mona's voice was
breathless with fear. "Oh, Rush, do you suppose— Is her
heart beating?"

"Of course it is, you idiot." Rush sounded angry but
he sounded scared too. "Here, help me."

He slung the limp little figure of Randy over his
shoulder and began to go downstairs. Cuffy had turned

on all the lights and opened all the windows. She had wasted no time. As they came down to the first floor hall they heard the screech of a siren as the emergency van drew up. In the vestibule, with the doors wide open, stood Cuffy in her red flannel wrapper with the grey tail of hair hanging down her back, and Oliver weeping drowsily in her arms.

"We can't wake Randy up!" cried Mona as Rush with a grunt of weariness put Randy on the floor. Very carefully he put her down. She looked so small and pale and seemed so fast asleep that he felt terribly frightened. Cuffy dropped the howling Oliver and bent over Randy.

"She'll be all right once she gets a little air, poor child."

The emergency men came in in their dark-blue uniforms. There seemed to be dozens of them, hundreds of them, thundering up and down stairs. Two of them worked over Randy. It didn't take long. In about five minutes she opened her eyes. "Rush," she whispered.

"Yes, Ran."

"What happened?"

"Coal gas. Something happened to the furnace but everything's okay."

"I dreamed you and I were going down a long dark tunnel like a subway tunnel only with no cars. Way in back of us, at the end, there was a lighted doorway. You kept saying, 'We ought to go back, we ought to go back,' but I kept saying, 'No, no, we ought to go on.'

This was so extraordinary that Rush could hardly believe it.

"I dreamed about that tunnel myself," he told Randy. "Only I saw Isaac in the doorway. And he was really there. He's the one who saved us, by barking so loud."

"Rush," said Cuffy, "after this you can keep that dog in your room every night if you want to. He can sleep on the foot of your bed, bury his bones under the living-room carpet, leave his muddy paw prints on the woodwork and anything else he likes. He's a wonderful dog and no mistake!"

Out of doors a little knot of curious people had gathered; the light shone on their wet umbrellas. Willy Sloper pushed his way among them, mounted the steps and entered. He had a piece of flannel around his neck, and his spiky hair glistened with rain.

"Where's your rubbers, Willy?" demanded Cuffy. Willy ignored the question.

"What happened?" he whispered strickenly. "Was it the furnace?"

"Coal gas. I don't know how it happened," replied Rush. "I put coal on the furnace myself before I went to bed. I left the furnace door wide open too."

"Open!" croaked Willy, almost with his normal voice. "You mean you left it open? Did'n I ever tell you you hafta leave that door shut? Some furnaces you leave the door open, some furnaces you leave the door shut. This one you hafta leave the door shut. Doggone it, didn't I ever tell you that?"

"I don't think so," Rush said humbly. "I just thought if you left the door open it would be better. More air and everything."

"My fault," whispered Willy tragically. "Doggone me for a dang old fool. Why, you mighta all been suffocatered in your beds. Pretty near was too, and I'd'a been to blame!"

Rush found himself whispering in sympathy. "Oh, that's all right, Willy. You probably did tell me and I forgot. Anyway I should have known: a fine engineer I'll make! And anyway we're all okay!"

"Dang old fool," muttered Willy to himself, shaking his head.

It was at that moment that Father's taxi drew up. At a quarter to four on Sunday morning he found himself greeted by an emergency van, a crowd of curious onlookers, and a policeman who didn't want to let him go into his own house. When he did go in he found dozens of other policemen, his entire family in the front hall attired in bathrobes and pajamas, and Willy Sloper, who drifted toward him like a ghost and whispered, "It's all my fault, Mr. Melendy."

"*What's* all your fault?" cried Father. "Why can't you speak up? What are you whispering for? What in the name of heaven *is* all this? What's been going on?"

Cuffy explained. Rush explained. Willy explained.

Isaac barked. Mona and Randy and Oliver sat in a pale solemn little cluster on the stairs.

"That furnace!" said Father. "Out she goes before the fall; I've stood enough from her. More than enough. Are you sure you're all all right?"

"I almost suffocatered," said Randy in a stately voice.

"But you feel all right now?"

"Yes, except my head hurts."

"Mine does too," said Mona, hoping she looked pale.

"I feel hungry," Oliver said.

"Well, let's all go down to the kitchen and get something to eat. Maybe it'll make us feel better. You come too, Willy. I'll just run down and take a look at the old villainess in the basement. I want to talk to the emergency men for a minute too." Father ran lightly down the stairs and the rest followed more slowly. There were rivulets and ponds of water under every window; the rugs were soaked, and the drawing-room curtains hung limp and damp. The house smelled of rain but it was a good smell. The serpent had been vanquished.

Father joined them in the kitchen.

"Randy, are those your clothes downstairs in the basement?" he asked, opening the icebox door.

"Oh, gee whiz! Yes, they are, Father."

"What are they doing down there? Even your shoes are tied to the clothesline."

"Well, I fell into the lake at Central Park this afternoon," began Randy. It all had to be explained.

"You've had quite a day, haven't you, Randy?" said Father when she had finished. He looked out the window at the retreating, screaming emergency van, and the slowly departing crowd of people who seemed disappointed that there had been no disaster. He looked at his disheveled family, and then he took a cold lamb chop out of the ice box and tossed the whole thing to Isaac.

"Be it ever so humble," said Father. "There's certainly no place like home."

"So what it's come to is this," Father told them the next day. He had called them all into the study. "We're going to have a new furnace; an oil one this time that can't cause so much trouble."

"But what about Willy Sloper?" interrupted Randy anxiously. "If we have an oil furnace, what will Willy do?"

Father smiled. "Don't you worry, Randy. There'll always be work for Willy in this house. He's practically a member of the family."

That was a relief to everyone.

"Now a new oil furnace costs at least two hundred dollars," continued Father. "I don't pay much more than that in rent every summer for the valley house. *This* house we own; it's ours. But though there's no rent there is a mortgage and there are taxes. In addition to that it needs new wallpaper, the roof has to be fixed, and the third-floor stairway has to be repaired before it goes down like a stack of dominoes. All that costs

money, and an authority on economics always seems
to be just as poor or a little poorer than other people.
It's going to be rather a struggle. What I'm trying to
tell you is this: we'll have to forget about the valley
this summer. I hate telling you you'll have to stay in
the hot city, but I don't know what else to do. Maybe
a couple of weeks at the shore in August. That's the
most I can promise."

There was an appalled silence.

"Well," Mona said at last, "other people do it. I
guess we can if they can."

"We have the yard," added Rush. "And the roof."

"And there's Central Park," said Randy. "And the
tops of busses, and the hose. We can cool off in the
hose."

"Oh, boy!" cried Oliver. "That's what I like! Cooling
off in the hose."

"Well, you're good kids," Father said. "There never
were any better ones. Cleaner, maybe, or quieter, but
never any better."

"And another thing," Randy said. "I'm president of
the I.S.A.A.C. so it's all right for me to suggest it. We
don't really need as much allowance as you give us.
Why, I bet we could get along fine on a quarter apiece,
couldn't we, kids? Except Oliver of course . . ."

"I can get along on a nickel," interrupted Oliver
stoutly.

"After all money isn't everything," said Randy, rather

proud of herself, as if she had made a remarkable discovery.

"You're good kids," repeated Father. He didn't seem to be able to think of anything else to say.

"Then there's the Pig if Necessary," offered Rush.

"The what?" Father looked startled.

"The pig bank in the Office," Rush explained. "It's got about a dollar and ninety-six cents in it. Maybe more by now. It's not much, of course, but if you could use it . . ."

"Oh. Oh, thanks, Rush," Father said. "But I don't think I'm reduced to that just yet. You keep it in case of emergency."

The first few days were fine; they all felt self-sacrificing and practiced economy with zeal. Every unnecessary light was turned off. The telephone was hardly ever used. They took all the empty ginger ale bottles back to the grocery, and went by the Good Humor man with their faces averted.

But by Thursday it became very hot. The ailanthus trees were in profuse full leaf. Through the open windows of the house drifted the myriad noises of other people's living: radios quacking away, typewriter keys pecking, dishes clashing together in sinks, voices talking, pianos being played, and a woman singer who practiced scales dutifully hour after hour, day after day.

"You know, Ran," Mona confided that day after school. "I keep thinking of the valley. Last night I dreamed about it. Do you remember the bobwhites? They say 'bob' and then take a deep breath and say 'white' afterwards."

"I know," said Randy. "And the mourning doves. The way they sound so far away even if they're right in the tree up above you. I love mourning doves, the whole summer in the valley always sounded of them."

Up in the Office, Rush was playing the piano. He started to thunder through the Revolutionary Etude as usual and then stopped.

"Nuts!" he exclaimed. Something had happened to a note in the middle register: it plinked like a guitar and ruined the whole effect. There was a pretty good piano in the valley house. "Oh, nuts, oh, nuts," repeated Rush unhappily, and closed the lid. And besides the piano there was a tennis court at the valley, and a dammed-up pool in the brook where they swam. The water was dark and tingling and cold; Randy said it was like swimming in iced root beer. And besides that there was the treehouse Rush had built in the beech tree, where no one else could come unless invited. There was the carpentry shop in the garage. There were the Sayles kids on the next farm who had a hayloft as big as a hotel ballroom, and horses to ride on, a mother who made the kind of pie you think of when you say the word "pie."

"Nuts!" repeated Rush. He went back to the piano, opened the lid, and crashed roughly down on the keys with his two closed fists. It made a good, loud, angry noise.

"What's the matter with you?" inquired Oliver, coming in. He was wearing an Indian war bonnet, and there were four cap pistols stuck in his belt.

"Oh, nothing." Rush closed the piano lid sheepishly. "Come on, Hiawatha, let's find something to do. We might rig up a wigwam for you in the back yard. Let's see if Cuffy will give us an old sheet."

"Boy!" commented Oliver enthusiastically, galloping out of the Office beside his brother on a nonexistent pinto pony.

Saturday was a day out of August by mistake. Not even the shades flapped in the open windows. In their economical mood the I.S.A.A.C. members had planned no excursion for themselves, and now they were sorry.

Randy lay on the floor. "I'm so bo-o-o-o-red!" she groaned, exactly as she had groaned on a wet Saturday many weeks before.

As if in reply the telephone downstairs began to ring. Nobody paid any attention; Cuffy always answered it, and it was probably for Father anyway.

"We might get on a subway and see how far it goes, and then get off and go exploring," suggested Mona. "It might go to Brooklyn, or Astoria, or the Bronx, or some other interesting place."

"Educational and inexpensive," agreed Rush without much enthusiasm. Lugubriously he began to play the

Chopin Funeral March for Randy's benefit. She adored funeral marches.

"Oh, Randy!" shouted Cuffy from downstairs.

"Yes, Cuffy?"

"Telephone, hurry."

"Telephone for me!" Randy sprang to her feet. "Oh, I hope it's something nice!"

"Probably just that bird-brain Dorothy Janeway wanting to gossip again," said Rush gloomily.

But it wasn't Dorothy Janeway this time. Randy came back looking pleased. She demonstrated her pleasure by a series of glissades and two high leaps.

"Do I remind you of Zorina?" she said.

"You remind me of a kangaroo," replied Rush absent-mindedly. "Come across, Randy. What was the telephone call about?"

"We're all going out for tea," she told him. "Mrs. Oliphant's invited us to have tea with her at the zoo."

"Even me?" asked Oliver, who was up to his ears in plasticine.

"Of course you too. All the I.S.A.A.C. members. You'll like it. Tea doesn't mean tea. It means ice cream."

"Well, that's a break," said Rush. "I like Mrs. Oliphant. When're we going?"

"Oh, in about an hour. Four o'clock she told me."

"I suppose we'll have to get cleaned up?" Rush said wistfully, gazing at the front of his shirt. It bore the marks of interesting encounters with chalk, maple syrup, machine oil, and good plain dirt.

"Oh, yes. Spick-and-span, of course. I'm even going to wear a hat. I wonder where my straw hat is? I haven't seen it since last summer."

Randy went leaping out of the room and they could hear her calling, "Cuffy, where's my straw ha-at?" And Cuffy's muffled answer from the kitchen, "My lands, child, I don't know. Did you look in the storeroom?"

Randy went into the storeroom and turned on the light, there were no windows. The place was full of things: winter clothes in mothproof bags, two old cribs, the family high chair, a couple of suitcases (though most of these were kept in the basement), everybody's ice skates, quantities of books and old magazines, stacks of framed pictures, and many other things including a sewing machine, and the stately dressmaker's form, size 40, that Cuffy built her dresses on.

Randy got so hot looking for her hat that she finally took off her dress and hung it up on the light bracket. By the time she discovered the hat she had discovered several other things as well: Cuffy's old pattern books, for instance, a forgotten Halloween costume, and a snapshot album full of pictures she wanted to look at.

Bearded with dust, wearing a petticoat and her straw hat, Randy at last emerged from the storeroom, her arms full. She banged the door shut behind her with her foot. Careless Randy. In the storeroom the electric light

burned brightly as before; and as the door slammed shut
a sudden draft lifted the wide collar of the dress she had
hung on the bracket and dropped it over the bulb.

"Cuffy," said Randy, coming down the stairs slowly,
"did you ever really wear clothes like the ones in this
pattern book?"

"What in heaven's name is all that truck?" inquired
Cuffy. "Here, let me look." She held the book far away
so that she could see it better. "Why that's not so long
ago. Nineteen hundred and twenty-six."

"Nineteen-twenty-*six!*" repeated Randy. "Even Mona
wasn't born *then!* Why, it's a terribly long time ago."

"Is it? Yes, I guess it is. Well, that's how we dressed.
Hats pulled down over our ears like they was football
helmets. Skirts up to the knee. Belts almost *down* to the
knee."

"Cuffy, even you?"

"Certainly me, why not?" said Cuffy haughtily "I
only weighed around a hundred and forty-six then."

"Well, I don't know how you could wear things like
that; I should think it would make you feel silly."

"You never can tell," said Cuffy. "Someday the
clothes you're wearing now will look just as outlandish
to you. Things change. Time changes 'em."

"Time," announced Rush, poking his head out the
door. "Time—marches ON!"

"March on yourself, my fine young man," scolded

Cuffy. "You can't go till you're clean, and you'll never get clean without you take a bath."

At last, radiant with scrubbing, wearing their best clothes and with the I.S.A.A.C. pins sparkling on their chests, they left the house. Upstairs in the closed storeroom there was only the faintest odor of hot cloth.

The bus ride was hot and horrible because all the top seats were taken, but once they got to Central Park everything was all right. Mrs. Oliphant met them wearing a flowered dress and a hat that Rush privately thought looked like an order of fruit salad.

The terrace of the restaurant was cool and shady and they sat under an umbrella and ate ice cream. In the pool below the terrace a sea lion floated peacefully with his hind flippers out, and another swam to and fro under the water emerging at regular intervals, blowing noisily, and disappearing again.

The Melendys told Mrs. Oliphant all about the coal gas experience. They all told her. It was really quite an important and interesting thing that had happened to them, now that it was over.

"But now we have to buy a new furnace, and a lot of other things, so we can't go to the country this summer, because we haven't got enough money," Randy told her expansively. Rush glowered at her and Mona gave her a kick under the table. Randy felt a hot red blush rising from her collarbone to the top of her head.

"Well, we *like* it, though," she added lamely. "We

really *like* staying here. There's the park, and the back yard, and rides on ferryboats and ever so many things to do even if we don't have as much allowance as we used—"

Rush kicked her this time; so hard that she couldn't help saying "Ouch." Mona changed the subject.

"Oh, Mrs. Oliphant," she was saying in an animated voice, "I *love* your bracelet. Isn't it *sweet?* Did it come from France?"

Usually Rush hated it when Mona acted like that. It always made him want to be tough and slangy by contrast. But today he was grateful to her. Mona could usually be counted on to save a situation, he had to admit that.

"No," Mrs. Oliphant said in her deep, old voice. "It came from Venice. My husband bought it for me in nineteen-eleven."

Randy went on eating her ice cream. It was so cool and comforting and delicious that by and by it cooled away the blush and she felt all right again.

In the closed storeroom at home the smell of burnt cloth was now very noticeable, but there was nobody there to smell it except a brindled old mouse who hastily departed to the second floor by a secret channel in the wall. In the collar of the dress that Randy had left on the bracket there was now a hole with brown fringed edges. It grew larger, second by second, the brown fringes writhed and curled; a tendril of blue smoke rose upward, and then all of a sudden there was a tiny flame licking and licking away at the collar.

"Nineteen-eleven," continued Mrs. Oliphant. "That must have been the year I met your father for the first time."

"Father! How old was he?" they cried.

"Oh, eleven or twelve. Bored to death he was. He'd been dragged all over Europe from museum to art gallery to cathedral. But I fixed that. I took him to Florian's in the Piazza San Marco and fed him ices, just as I'm feeding them to you, only instead of seals to look at there were pigeons, thousands of them, tame as a barnyard full of hens. And I took him riding in gondolas, and I introduced him to a family of other American children who were visiting there. The littlest girl was named Nora; she was only three or four and always tagging about and getting in the way. I remember your father said to me, 'Anybody under six years old should be kept in a cage.' The funny thing is that years later he married her!"

"Mother!" they cried.

"What did she look like then?" Randy asked.

"Like Mona, rather, only of course much littler. She had very large dark eyes, and a tangle of yellow curls and she wore a huge ribbon bow on her hair. When she grew up she looked hardly any different except that she no longer wore a bow."

Upstairs in the storeroom at home Randy's dress was

blazing cheerfully. Hungrily the flames reached out, and caught at the succulent folds of the mothproof bag that contained Father's dress suit. Soon that was blazing too.

Mrs. Oliphant set down her teacup, and looked at them. "Do you know that I own a lighthouse?" she inquired suddenly.

"A lighthouse?" repeated Randy. She had a picture of Mrs. Oliphant polishing the lenses of a giant lamp, and directing its rays to the storm-tossed ships at sea.

"At least it *was* a lighthouse," Mrs. Oliphant corrected herself. "And everything is there but the light. The tower and the house and the ocean and the rocks."

"A lighthouse to live in; that sounds neat," Rush said.

"It *is* neat," agreed Mrs. Oliphant. "Why don't you all come and spend the summer in it? It's a big place and there's plenty of room now that my children are grown and married. There's still room for them when they come to visit, as well as room for you. You can live in the tower."

"In the lighthouse itself?" Rush's eyes were glowing. So were Mona's and Randy's and Oliver's.

"In the lighthouse itself," replied Mrs. Oliphant.

"But isn't it—I mean, wouldn't it be a-a-an imposition?" said Mona uncomfortably.

"I knew and loved both your father and mother from the time they were children," said Mrs. Oliphant. "And it would give me great pleasure to have *their* children with me in my lighthouse. There! Does that sound as if I were being imposed upon?"

"No, I suppose it doesn't," Mona admitted.

"And when I get tired of you I'll lock you all up in the tower with nothing to eat but bread and water. Or maybe milk and a jar of Mrs. Wilkins's cookies. I'll telephone your father this very evening and see what he has to say about it."

At home at that moment Father came bursting out of his study. He lifted up his nose and sniffed.

"Cuffy!" shouted Father. "What's burning?"

Cuffy came out of the kitchen drying her hands on her apron. "Burning, Mr. Melendy? Why, nothing down here. I'm just . . ." She looked up the stairway at him and then beyond. Her eyes opened wide. "Oh, my lands, Mr. Melendy! Look upstairs! It must be fire!"

Isaac began to bark as Father raced up the stairs with Cuffy panting and thumping behind him. Above the noise they could hear an ominous crackling and snapping as they reached the top floor.

The Melendy children walked to Fifth Avenue with Mrs. Oliphant. They walked very slowly so that they wouldn't spoil the lovely coolness inside them created by the ice cream. Randy was hanging onto one of the old lady's arms and Oliver was hanging onto the other. Mona was carrying her knitting bag. Rush was just walking along monopolizing the conversation.

"Gee, I always thought it would be swell to live in a

lighthouse," he was saying. "From the first time I ever saw one when I was five years old. I bet the swimming's keen too, isn't it?"

"Yes, the swimming is extremely keen," said Mrs. Oliphant. She said it just at the very second that Father was shouting to Cuffy to call up the Fire Department. "And tell them to hurry!" he told her.

Mrs. Oliphant said good-bye to them at Sixty-fourth Street and they got on a bus going downtown. There were plenty of top seats, now, and a wind that was almost cool rose up to meet them as the bus jolted and bucked along the Avenue.

"Oh, boy, what a break!" Rush kept saying. "Wouldn't it be swell if Father said yes!"

"Do you think she really meant it?" Randy asked.

"I suppose so," Mona said. "After you told her we were practically paupers what else could she do? It's charity, that's what it is."

"Well, so what's the matter with charity?" Rush said unexpectedly. "Don't you think it's dumb to say no out of some sort of cockeyed pride when somebody you like *wants* to give you a present that you want to take? She likes us and we like her. She has a lighthouse and no one to appreciate it, now her kids are all grown up. I don't see anything wrong with that. I think it's swell and I think she *is* too."

"I do too," Randy said wholeheartedly. Rush was wonderful, she thought.

"And as for being paupers, we're not!" he went on. "Any man with a house and four children and a dog and a housekeeper and furnaceman has to be a millionaire to be rich. Well, we're not rich by a long shot. But neither are we paupers."

"All right," said Mona meekly. "I believe you."

After they got off the bus they walked through the street almost to their own block before they saw the fire engines.

"A fire!" yelped Rush joyfully, breaking into a run. They all ran with him; Mona holding onto Oliver's jacket to keep him from dashing into the street.

"My gosh, I think it's *our house!*" croaked Rush.

"I think so too," said Mona. And Randy began to cry. She couldn't help it.

"Where's Cuffy?" asked Oliver bouncing along beside Mona. "Will they have to carry her down a ladder, do you think?"

"Oh, be still, Oliver, and quit bawling, Ran," ordered Rush. "Look, one of the engines is going away, everything's probably all right. You don't see any smoke, do you? You don't see any fire?"

"There's Father now!" gasped Randy gladly, and she raced right past a policeman, two firemen, and up the steps into Father's arms. "What happened, what happened?" cried Randy, her arms tight around him. "Are you all right? Really?"

"I'm all right, and Cuffy's all right." .

"Is Isaac all right?" Rush asked breathlessly.

"We're all all right. There was a small fire in the store-room, that's all. It's out now. We can't imagine how it started. Do any of you have an idea?"

Nobody had any. Randy kept her arms around Father, feeling weak with relief.

"None of you went in there today, did you? Didn't leave a light burning, or anything?" queried a fireman who had been talking to Father.

Randy backed away from her father suddenly. "*I* was there," she said in a horrified voice. "I don't remember if I turned the light off. Maybe I didn't. Could that have done it?"

"Sure could, sister," said the fireman. "Bad wiring, or maybe something was hanging too close to the bulb."

"My dress!" moaned Randy. "I hung my dress on the light while I was looking for my hat. It's all my fault!" And she began to cry again.

"First coal gas, then a fire, and now a flood!" said Father exasperatedly. "The harm's done, and it's too late to wail about it, Randy. Perhaps next time you'll be more careful, that's all; not go about hanging your clothes over light bulbs in that extraordinary way. Your winter coat and my dress suit, the high chair, and a set of Thackeray seem to be about all that's gone. The storeroom is a mess: charred black, soaking wet, and they've chopped the wall full of holes: had to. But I'm covered by insurance, luckily."

"Well, that's a break anyway," said Rush, for the third time that day. Then he turned to Randy. "Remember I was the one who left the furnace door open when we almost suffocated," he comforted her. "You're no worse than I am."

Pale and chastened Randy helped Cuffy with the dishwashing after dinner. Willy Sloper was bringing barrels of debris down from the storeroom. When Randy set out the empty milk bottles in the areaway she saw something she hadn't expected, somehow. Regal and imposing even in its state of charred ruin, Cuffy's dressmaker's form stood in lonely distinction beside the garbage can and the trash barrels.

"Oh, Cuffy, did *that* get burned too?"

"Never you mind, my lamb," Cuffy said. "For about a year now, I've been too stout to get into a size forty, and that dress form's been kind of on my conscience. Now, thank goodness, I won't have to reduce!"

SCHOOL was over. The school books were dumped on the Office table for the last time. By and by somebody would stuff them into the already crowded bookcase, and no one would ever look at them except by accident, years later. There would be Randy's French grammar all scrawled with drawings of sorceresses and a question in her handwriting on the fly leaf that said "Nancy Curtin est nuts, n'est-ce-pas?" and a reply written by her friend Dorothy Janeway that said "Et comment!" There would be Mona's English history with the name Mona Melendy written in nine different handwritings, all her own: she couldn't decide which would look most distinguished as an autograph. There would be Rush's algebra full of businesslike notations and diagrams of airplanes: Curtiss P.40's, and Hudson Bombers.

"The day school is out is my favorite day next to my birthday," Randy said.

"My favorite day is going to be next Saturday," said

Rush. For when Father had agreed to accept Mrs. Oliphant's wonderful invitation, Randy had said, "*Please can we leave on Saturday?*" They had all felt that it was very important to the I.S.A.A.C. for them to leave on a Saturday. So it had been arranged, and now Saturday was only two days away.

All over the house suitcases gaped open hungrily and two ancient trunks were slowly being fed, bit by bit: delicious morsels such as Oliver's overalls, Mona's party dress, assorted bathing suits, six pairs of sneakers, Beethoven's Sonatas, the Milk of Magnesia, the iodine, three rolls of adhesive tape, litters of socks and scores of other things. The trunks had been in the family for years and years and were encrusted with labels from far places.

"Hotel de Russie, Rome," read Randy, pausing with an armful of pajamas.

"Mussolini!" said Cuffy, coming out of the steamer trunk with a red face.

"Hotel Savoy, London," read Randy.

"Bombs," said Cuffy sadly. "Blackouts."

"Hotel Adlon, Berlin," read Randy.

"That Hitler!" said Cuffy indignantly, and dived back into the trunk. "Them Nazis!"

Randy stopped reading labels.

"What was it like when the world was peaceful, Cuffy?"

"Ah," said Cuffy, coming up again. "It seemed like a lovely world; anyway on top where it showed. But it didn't last long. First there was a long, bad war, and then peace like the ham in a sandwich, and now a long, bad war again. It was nice when you could go any place; on boats and trains to furrin cities. I went with your mother and father when Mona was a baby. I guess I wheeled Mona's baby buggy through most of the parks in Europe. They call 'em gardens over there. Borghese Gardens, Luxembourg Gardens, Kensington Gardens. Real pretty they was, all of 'em; and nice little children too, even if they couldn't talk American. Let's see now what did I do— Run upstairs, Randy, and see if Oliver's rubber boots are in his closet."

A thumping and banging was heard, and Oliver entered dragging his tricycle and the old rocking horse behind him.

"Cuffy, will you please put these in the trunk?" said Oliver. And Randy fled, as the storm clouds gathered.

At last it was Saturday. The express men, smelling of crates, and wearing caps on the backs of their heads and pencils behind their ears, had taken away the trunks. The taxi drivers and Father and Willy Sloper and Rush took the rest of the luggage down to the two waiting taxis. It was interesting luggage. Besides a rare accumulation of elderly suitcases and hatboxes, there were several cardboard boxes, a duffel bag, a tricycle (Oliver had won out on that but lost on the rocking horse), two umbrellas and a walking stick bound together, some steamer rugs and the special suitcase with a window that contained the melancholy Isaac.

"All you folks need is a baby buggy and a bird cage," Willy Sloper said. He stood sadly waving after them.

The two taxis bulging with children and luggage soon drew up at the station. Father, Mona, and Oliver burst out of one. Cuffy, Randy, and Rush burst out of the other, Rush carrying Isaac's suitcase carefully. They made quite a procession across the station.

On the train they got seats in the day coach. It smelled of soot and oranges and plush and babies. For, of course, there was a baby (just like Miss Pearl said, Mona thought) and he was tuning up for a good cry. Father kissed them all good-bye, distributed chocolate bars among them, and promised to join them the next day.

Out on the platform a voice suddenly bellowed something that sounded like "AW-BAW!" and a few seconds later the train quivered, drew itself together, and stepped out upon its track. Oliver got chocolate all over the windowpane trying to get a last glimpse of Father, and Cuffy mopped her hot face with her best handkerchief. Mona started reading her book almost at once so that the other passengers would realize that travel was nothing new to her, but Randy stared out the window frankly interested. As for Rush, he surreptitiously opened the suitcase beside him and gave Isaac a piece of chocolate. Just to prove that they were still friends.

The conductor was a nice man.

"Hot enough for you?" he asked them as he punched the tickets.

"We won't be hot very long," Oliver told him. "We're going to live in a lighthouse."

"Sonny, next to an iceberg I can't think of any place I'd rather live just now."

"Why do conductors always look like that, I wonder?" Mona said to Rush when he'd gone. "Conductors all have the same face. Two lines going down their cheeks, pointed noses, and glasses. They are never very fat. They're usually quite kind."

"Maybe for the same reason that all policemen have the same kind of face," Rush said. "Wide and pink, like a baked ham."

After a while the train plunged into the country. Real country with great dignified trees in full leaf like the trees in paintings by old masters, and rambler roses pouring thick as lava over walls and fences. When the train stopped at stations the Melendys saw brown-skinned children piling out of station wagons, or running along the platform to meet somebody.

"I can't wait, I can't wait!" cried Randy.

"It'll be soon now," Cuffy told her calmly. "Just hold your horses."

The day coach was oven-hot, particles of soot crept under the closed windows and stuck to clothes and damp skin. The baby was going full blast, and now and then Isaac uttered a high-pitched yelp of sympathy.

An hour went by, and the country began to change: there were fewer trees now, and the train crossed a bridge across a long still strip of water where empty dories, and little snub-nosed launches lay motionless like the castoff slippers of a giantess.

"Kettle Ne-eck!" bawled the conductor suddenly; and the Melendy children sat up and took notice, because they knew that Kettle Neck was where they got off. Cuffy bustled about, sorting out belongings, and scrubbing at soot and chocolate on faces with a damp handkerchief.

"There's Mrs. Oliphant," she said as the train slowed down. "She's there waiting for us. Randy, pull your hat forward. Oliver, remember to shake hands with your right hand."

When they got off the train the air was almost cool and it smelled of clams. "Queek queek," mewed a sea gull high overhead.

Mrs. Oliphant was very glad to see them. She wore a suit made out of pongee, a hat with a green veil, an amethyst necklace, a lapis lazuli necklace, and a silver one with her eyeglasses on it. She seemed unperturbed by the amount of luggage that appeared with the Melendys. "Come, children," she said. "Somehow we must get this all into the Motor." That was what she always called it, the Motor, with a capital M.

The station agent, a man named Mr. Bassett, helped them with the luggage. When Rush saw the Motor he almost dropped everything he was carrying. It was an ancient station wagon which sat very high and narrow on its wheels. The original windows, broken long ago, had been replaced by regular four-pane windows like those you see in sheds. Rush thought the Motor looked more live a traveling greenhouse than a station wagon.

"Fifteen years I've had it," Mrs. Oliphant told them proudly. "Climb in, children. Cuffy, you and Oliver sit in front with me."

Rush took Isaac out of his bag and held him on his lap. Mrs. Oliphant turned on the ignition and off they went. She drove like a queen, sitting very straight, glancing graciously from left to right and traveling all the while at the perilous speed of eleven miles an hour. The Motor coughed and thumped, and the exhaust filled the car with horrible fumes, "worse than coal gas," Mona whispered. After fifteen minutes of it they all felt slightly nauseated. But only slightly.

The motor turned from the main road through a little wood, took another turn between two gateposts, struggled up a small rise and emerged at the summit with its last gasp.

"Gee whiz!" exclaimed Randy, and Rush just gave a long, low whistle. It was hard to imagine anything better. The lighthouse had once been an honest-to-goodness lighthouse, no doubt about that. It was round and stout and tall, with a wide red band around its middle. The small house at its base had been added to many times so that it was now ample and rambling. Beyond it a narrow brilliant garden descended to smooth elephant-colored bands of rock. Beyond the rock was the sea, clear as blue glass and dotted with small rocky islands like islands painted on a Chinese screen. A pier extended from the nearest rocks and at its end lay tethered a cat-boat and a dinghy. There were some wind-twisted pines in the garden, and from the branches of one hung a swing. On the low roof of the house a yellow cat lay fast asleep, and on the lawn a great Dane posed like an iron dog. The place had everything!

"What's the dog's name, Mrs. Oliphant?" said Rush, holding onto Isaac.

"Hamlet. He's very gentle."

"What's the cat's name?" asked Randy.

"Butter. On account of her color."

"Are the boats ours too? Yours, I mean?" asked Oliver.

"Yes, the boats are ours too. You must learn to sail this summer." She said it as if she were telling them they must learn Latin declensions or something.

"Boy!" cried Oliver, flinging open the door of the Motor and tumbling out on the grass. Isaac tumbled out after him barking joyously and careening in mad enthusiastic circles around the stately Hamlet.

A man in blue denim came to help carry luggage. His

sleeves were rolled up and there was a Chinese dragon tattooed on one forearm.

"This is Wilkins," said Mrs. Oliphant introducing them, "and, Wilkins, these are Mona and Randy and Rush and Oliver. You must teach them how to sail, pull them out of the water when they start to drown, and keep them out of mischief generally."

"Yes'm, Mrs. O, I'd be gladta. Sure would." Wilkins smiled and picked up the two heaviest suitcases as if they'd been sofa cushions. The dragon on his forearm rippled over the swelling muscle, that was all. They knew they were going to like him a lot.

"Is that what he calls you . . . Mrs. O?" whispered Randy as Mrs. Oliphant opened the front door.

"Yes, Wilkins had trouble with the word Oliphant. He likes all words and names to be as brief as possible. Yep. Nope. Okay. Sure do. That's the way he likes it. So I'm called Mrs. O."

The house was a good house. The living room was big with a low ceiling and a lot of things on the walls, shelves of books and statues and pictures and mirrors and French fans under glass, and peacock feathers in a copper vase.

"Look at that!" said Rush, standing still; both his arms pulled down by suitcases. He was staring at a piano. It was the real McCoy all right: a Steinway parlor grand, black and shining as wet tar, with all its ivory keys gleaming in a sort of elegant smile.

"Just take a look at that," repeated Rush in a dreamy voice.

"You must play on it whenever you wish," Mrs. Oliphant told him comfortably. "Now, then, here is the dining room and here is the kitchen. This is Mrs. Wilkins, who does our cooking for us. She makes the best cookies you ever ate."

"Cuffy, I like this place, don't you?" said Oliver in his clear little voice. They all laughed, and Mrs. Wilkins wiped her floury hands on her apron and shook hands with each of them. She was sort of young, like Wilkins, with black hair and red cheeks.

Then Mrs. Oliphant showed them the lighthouse. It was wonderful. You went up a corkscrew staircase, and there, one above the other, were two round rooms each with two cots and an old-fashioned washstand. White muslin curtains flapped at the windows. Above the bedrooms was the sunroom. It was very small with windows all the way around, and a window seat underneath that, and a bookcase under that with old books in it: The Heir of Redclyffe, Hans Brinker, Jules Verne, Macé's Fairy Tales, and a whole set of Louisa M. Alcott written in French!

"Dibs on the room just under this one for Mona and me," said Randy with great presence of mind. "I never saw such a wonderful place as this in my whole life!"

"Where's Cuffy going to sleep?" asked Oliver, suddenly anxious.

"In the house. I'll hear you if you say my name out the window," Cuffy told him.

From their tower the Melendys could see the world around them in a circle. Sky with sea gulls in it and nothing else except a patch of those tiny silvery clouds that look like the scales of a carp. In one direction there was a feathering of green trees, and in the other the clear still sea, stirred only in one spot with a dappling of ripples. The waves made a silky lapping against the rocks.

"Let's go swimming," said Rush suddenly. "Mrs. Oliphant, could we go swimming?"

And in no time at all the Melendys were hurling themselves into the water. It was colder than it looked and Randy yelped like a seal. Oliver plowed prudently to and fro at the edge, with buckets of sand and water to build a fort with. Mona and Rush swam far out.

"I like Mrs. Oliphant, don't you?" Mona said.

"I like everything," Rush told her. "The piano, and the lighthouse, and what's-his-name with the dragon on his arm, and the whole works."

Mona turned over and floated. The sky was blue in the middle and honey-colored around the edges; the patch of little clouds was swimming away toward the horizon. She felt water oozing slowly up under her bathing cap behind her ears, but she didn't care because there were no more curls to worry about. Someday I'm going to be grown up, Mona thought suddenly. Going on fourteen is pretty old after all. Pretty soon now I'll be really grown up, with a permanent wave, and a lot of responsibilities like trying to earn a living, and becoming a great actress. It all seemed very close and frightening, suddenly, and she turned over and swam the crawl as fast as she could out to sea. Fast, with her feet churning and her arms reaching until she had left the knowledge of her advancing age far behind. After a while she turned over and floated again, resting. The lighthouse looked like a toy, and she could hear Rush yelling, "Come back, Mona, you dope." When she did start back she hurried, because now beneath her she could see dark large shadows. Were they moving, coming after her? Could they be sharks? Mona flailed with her legs and reached with her arms, speeding through the water. She was enjoying her panic, because deep down in her mind she was serenely aware that the dark shadows were nothing but eelgrass.

Randy walked along the rocks exploring. Her knees and elbows were lavender, her teeth chattering, and she was covered with gooseflesh; but as long as Cuffy didn't know it Randy could ignore it. She came to a little pool full of sea water and kneeled down shivering, to ex- amine it. She saw barnacles, and seaweed, and blue- black mussels, and some tiny turreted shells that wob- bled decorously across the floor of the pool. When she reached down and picked one up to find out what made it wobble all she could see was the tip end of a minute pink claw. She dropped it back again, and lay down on her stomach to get a better view of this small busy world.

She saw a big crusty old villain of a crab waltzing sideways through the weeds, and some little fish that would hang motionless and nearly invisible in the water for minutes at a time and then dart quickly as if pulled by threads. The longer she looked the larger the world of the pool became, until it was a jungle ravine full of wild beasts and sudden dangers.

Rush was trying to make Isaac come swimming, but he wouldn't for a long time. He ran up and down the pier yapping.

"Come on, boy, come on!" bellowed Rush frantically. "Don't be a sissy!" It would be terrible to have a dog that was a sissy about the sea.

Isaac ran down the pier again and back to the edge. Hamlet ambled along the pier, took one disgusted look at Isaac and dived into the water. That was too much for Isaac. Shamed into it, he gathered himself together and plunged into the hated element which had always meant baths to him.

Oliver was scooped up from his earthworks by Cuffy and carried away to supper in the kitchen with Mrs. Wilkins.

The older ones had supper on the terrace later with Mrs. Oliphant. They looked very clean with their wet hair and salt-scoured faces. A whole flock of freckles had already alighted on Randy's nose, and Rush said he thought he must be sunburned because he could feel his back; usually he hardly knew it was there.

"Gee, Mrs. Wilkins, you're certainly a very fine cook," Rush said, turning to look at her. "This is the best blueberry pie I ever ate, and I'm kind of a connoisseur."

"He ought to be; he once ate a whole pie and a half by himself. A whole rhubarb one and half of an apple one. At eleven o'clock in the morning he did it," said Randy, proud of his achievement.

Afterwards they all went and sat in the living room. Cuffy darned, Mrs. Oliphant knitted, and Randy held the wool for her. Hamlet and Isaac lay side by side on the rug, stretched out flat without even the flicker of a paw, in the manner of dogs who are exhausted by the all important barking and running they have done during the day. Mona had found a wonderful new book called *Under Two Flags*, and she was reading it. As for Rush, he cast so many longing glances at the piano that Mrs. Oliphant finally said, "Well, why in the world don't you go and play us something?"

So Rush did. It was a swell piano with a tone like purple velvet. First he played the Bach Chaconne, and then the Brahms Intermezzo, the one that sounds like dancing, and then, because he was showing off, he tore into the Revolutionary Etude, and Randy sat holding her breath waiting for the terrible mistake he always

made in the same place. But it never came! She let out
her breath in a sigh of relief.

"Bravo!" said Mrs. Oliphant, picking up a stitch.
"You'll be a very good pianist someday if you work
hard."

It wasn't Randy's idea of much of a compliment. She
privately thought Rush would be able to knock the spots
off any pianist from Josef Hofmann down; but Rush
seemed pleased.

Now that he had demonstrated how good he was, he
played all the simple things they asked for, and then
Mrs. Oliphant dug out an old dog-eared book of songs,
and they sang "Sweet and Low" (with Cuffy booming a
sturdy alto), and "Oh, Susanna," and "Camptown
Races," and "Funiculi Funicula," and they finished with
"The Star-Spangled Banner." They all stood up to sing
it; and Randy made even the dogs stand up. On this
splendid note the evening ended. Mrs. Oliphant stuffed
her knitting into a large crimson bag, the dogs were
banished to the kitchen, and all the good nights said.

"Listen," whispered Rush, as they entered the lighthouse. "Let's go up to the top and look out."

Tiptoeing up the corkscrew stair they went through
the boys' room, where Oliver lay asleep with the sheet
kicked off and his arms and legs flung out like the letter
X, and on up through the girls' room to the little room
at the top.

"It's the moon room instead of the sun room now,"

Randy said. It was true. The place was flooded with the bluish radiance of moonlight. Out of doors ten thousand glittering icy flames licked at the waves, and in the sky all except the most brilliant stars were drowned in light.

"Well, here we are," said Rush. "Thanks to you, Randy, and the I.S.A.A.C. You know I think maybe I'm going to like this even better than the valley."

"That was a swell idea of yours, Randy," Mona told her. "Just think, if it hadn't been for the I.S.A.A.C. Rush would never have found Isaac, and you wouldn't have made friends with Mrs. Oliphant, and we wouldn't have been here at all!"

"And you would still have been bearing the burden of those pigtails," Rush told her. "No, but really, it *is* sort of funny when you think about it. Everything important happened on a Saturday. Of course, the coal gas was really Sunday morning . . ."

"Well, it *began* on Saturday," Randy insisted.

"We won't need a club down here," Mona said.

"Or any allowance," agreed Rush. "Not with all that ocean and the boats and everything."

"Let's keep it for fall, and then when we go back we can begin again."

"We might do good deeds with it," Randy said. She was so happy that she wanted to do something about it. Perform a noble action or give a present to somebody, or be good for the rest of her life. Of course, when the opportunity came she would go down before temptation as soon as anyone else, but just now she didn't believe it.

They leaned their arms on the window sill and looked at the world; so changed, so beautiful, in this strange light. The water lapped and purred against the rocks, and the breeze that cooled their faces smelled of honeysuckle and salt marshes.

"Now it's going to be Saturday every day all summer long," said Randy, and yawned a wide, peaceful, happy yawn.